COMEBACK

COMEBACK

A Novel

CRAIG STROHM

PELICAN POND

Published by Pelican Pond Publishing,
Fine Fiction for All Ages,
an imprint of Blue Dolphin Publishing, Inc.

For inquiries or orders, please address
Blue Dolphin Publishing, Inc.
P.O. Box 8, Nevada City, CA 95959
1-800-643-0765
www.bluedolphinpublishing.com/PelicanPond/

ISBN: 1-57733-096-X

Library of Congress Cataloging-in-Publication Data

Strohm, Craig, 1951-
    Comeback : a novel / Crag Strohm.
        p. cm.
    ISBN 1-57733-096-X
    1. Motion picture producers and directors—Fiction.
2. Basketball coaches—Fiction. 3. Basketball players—
Fiction. 4. Fathers and sons—Fiction. I. Title.

PS3619.T76 C6 2001
813'.6—dc21

                                                2001034346

Cover design: LeeAnn Brook Design

Printed in the United States of America

    10   9   8   7   6   5   4   3   2   1

For Big Chum and the G-man

"I have fought the good fight, I have finished the race,
I have kept the faith."

2 Timothy 4:7

ACKNOWLEDGMENTS

Thanks to all the players who were either willingly or unwillingly played a part in my biggest yarn to date. You know how I love to mix the truth with a little of my own interpretive embellishment. The trick, of course, is not revealing where one ends and the other begins. I sincerely hope I managed to gray that area enough so I haven't offended anyone; the similarities between real people and fictitious ones was purely *not* coincidental. Hey,

NO HARM, NO FOUL!

There were some very special players along the way that helped me turn dreams into reality and I would like to give them some special recognition.

Coaches Awards: Louise Mcfadden
Ryan Curry
Peter Collier

Most Inspirational: The Lady Miners (past, present, future)
Pastor Dick
The Fightin' Mags
Those Lakewood Cheeseheads

MVP: Lady Di

The start of any successful athletic campaign must begin with a vivid imagination, ardent desire, unbending enthusiasm, sincere belief and a strong foundation of fundamentals. I also found that to be true about writing.

CHAPTER ONE

MARCH 19, 1988

SATURDAY

STATE CHAMPIONSHIPS

OAKLAND COLISEUM

It was a play they practiced many times during the regular season.

Usually the team worked on special situation plays at the end of every practice. Coach Peterson liked to work on the team's special plays when the team was tired. It was in the fourth quarter when games were won and lost. It was then that you needed the most composure, the most concentration.

Most of Coach's special situations plays were secret ones that he never used during the game so the opposing coach couldn't smell them out. The only problem with that was the team rarely got a chance to use them beforehand in a game situation. That was the case with the play the Empire High Lady Warriors were about to run. They had never run it in a game.

But here it was, three seconds left, down by two, and Coach Peterson was yelling "two for three," "two for three," at the top of his lungs in hopes he might be heard across the arena floor. Two for three was the code for Coach's "out-of-bounds-underneath-your-own-basket-no-time-on-the-clock-no-time-outs special secret play."

1

Coach Peterson was always conservative when it came to using time-outs. Painstaking careful about preserving them. Always trying to hang on to them in case they might be needed for "end of game situations."

But the Warriors had none left.

Coach had used them all early in the game trying to slow Mater Dei's early onslaught. An early onslaught it was too, with the Mater Dei Monarchs leading twenty-two to six after just one quarter.

It had certainly looked like Coach wouldn't be needing any last second secret specials, but the Warriors had battled their way back, never leading in the game but finally getting within two points when the Warrior point guard Jennifer Kelly buried their eleventh three-pointer of the game with forty-two seconds left. That forced the Monarchs to throw up a shot with three seconds remaining on the thirty second shot clock.

The Warriors rebounded, hit the outlet and raced down court.

They never flinched.

There was no hesitation.

Coach had always told them there would be no time-outs called in that situation.

Just get open and fire away.

The first open shot was always a good shot, according to Coach Peterson.

"Swish Happens" was one of his favorite sayings.

It didn't matter anyway because with less than fifteen seconds left, the Warriors finally had hope, but they didn't have any time-outs.

Kelly weaved the ball through the middle and the Warriors two long ball launching wings sprinted the outside lanes. Caitlin Cook was on the left and Angie Rodriguez on the right. Both of them heading straight for the three-point arc.

Cook got there first, but Kelly was still dribbling through transition traffic.

Kelly's head was up, and she was desperately searching for a spot up shooter.

Hoping Kelly would spot her, Cook took her arriving defender down in the key and then V-cut back to the three-point arc.

The timing was perfect.

Kelly hit her with a bullet, a crisp one handed pass off the dribble. Cook turned and squared up to the basket.

It was a driveway dream shot.

A game winner. The shot you play over and over in your mind when you're growing up, and spending hours outside your house grooving your shot.

Everyone watching in the Oakland Coliseum lifted off their backsides and collectively sucked the air out of the arena!

It was right on line. It looked good. It had a chance.

It was short.

It clanged off the front of the rim.

That was the bad news. The good news was it also clanged off of one of Mater Dei's giant post players and flew out of bounds.

Warrior's ball underneath.

The play was a simple little stack inbound play. The deception was that the Warriors didn't use any other stack inbound plays. It could be used against a man or zone defense, and the Warriors had practiced it against both.

The point guard, Kelly, would be the inbound passer. The right wing Rodriguez would be the first player in the stack and clear to the close corner. The left wing, Cook, would be the next in line. She would step to the ball and then turn and go to the top of the arc. The two Warrior posts, Emily Bridge and Stacy Renfrow, would be next in line. When the ball was slapped they would set a double screen for Cook heading back to the arc. Hopefully one of them would connect with Cook's defender, and the screen would free the shooter. The ball was to be lobbed to the top of the key for a three-point attempt.

Coach Peterson had no qualms about shooting three-pointers for game winners, even when they weren't necessary. Even before the inception of the three-point shot a couple of years ago, he had his teams attempt many game winners from long range.

Some were successful and some were not. He was prepared to live with that.

From the outside Coach Peterson looked the same as he always looked at this point of a game.

His knit tie knot was twisted and hung inches below his top button, which of course had been undone even before tip-off. His khaki slacks bagged at the knees and bunched up on the top of his bark colored Skechers.

Top to bottom he was dressed in clothes his wife had purchased at a Sacramento mall a few weeks before the season started.

Coach always wanted new duds for every season, but he hated shopping. Hated going to the mall. This year he had informed his wife that he was going for the preppie look, although he and his wife knew he was twenty-five years and twenty-five pounds past preppie.

His outfits had been laundered numerous times during the season trying to exorcise the perspiration and burger special sauce. At this point of the season Coach knew the win loss record of all his shirts, ties, and trousers. Some ties had already been benched and would never see any playing time again.

Tonight Coach was wearing his best record. His luckiest clothes.

Although Coach Peterson dressed in a similar fashion night after night, on the inside, things were much different than the previous thirty-five games they had played that season.

On the inside he was a Hindu, a Yogi, Mohandas Gandhi. He was as calm as he had ever been for a game, especially a game this season.

This season there had been a great deal of high expectations.

The Warriors were the preseason number one pick in the *Sacramento Bee*. They were expected to win their league, probably win the section and contend for the NorCal championship.

The Warriors had met those expectations and surpassed them. They beat Lincoln High of Stockton for the section title. Then they toppled Archbishop Mitty of San Jose, then mighty Berkeley to win the Northern California Championship. Berkeley had been rated number ten in the nation by *USA Today*.

Nobody expected the Warriors to be playing for the state title.

Those early expectations put a tremendous amount of pressure on the team and on the coaching staff.

But the Warriors had made it. Farther than anyone could have expected, they had exceeded anyone's predictions. The season was already the most successful basketball campaign in the school's history. Boys or girls.

And since it was a consensus that this crusade was already deemed an enormous success, there was absolutely no pressure to win this game.

Everyone was having fun. Enjoying the moment.

The players, coaches, parents, teachers, administrators, student body, and the entire community in the Northern California town of Empire was enjoying the ride.

Maybe it was because of the lack of pressure that Coach was having such a great game. He was coaching the best game of his life in the biggest game of his life. Each adjustment he made, each play he called was determined quickly and with complete clarity.

It was just him. Alone. Complete focus.

He was in the zone.

He was in the zone because he was able to completely let go of the outcome. The outcome simply didn't matter. And the fact that he was exhausted, constipated, and his immune system was a quart low, didn't matter either.

Coach was on a roll.

The referee handed the ball to Kelly.
Immediately Rodriguez cleared. Cook took her step toward Kelly and then spun and headed for the top of the key. Bridge missed Cook's defender, but not Renfrow.
Renfrow nailed her.
She knocked Cook's defender back into the key. Kelly lobbed it. It was a little high, but Cook reached up and gathered it in. She set her feet and fired it. As it left Cook's hand it looked like it had too much arc. Cook's defender had begun to recover, but Cook had plenty of time to get the shot off.

Why so much arch? Too much arch on the ball! It's too high! It's a rainbow! She had plenty of time. Why had she hurried it?

Coach never saw it come down.

For the last twenty-one seasons, even during Coach's short stint as the boy's coach, Wilson "Willie" Dutroy had been Coach's assistant. He always sat closest to the scorer's table and kept readily needed stats: things like players' fouls, time-outs left and points scored by opposing players. Stats Coach needed in a hurry to make adjustments or alter strategy. In those twenty-one seasons Coach Dutroy had learned his role. As Coach Peterson's assistant, you offer encouragement and re- mind players of assignments, but you never sub, never criticize an official, and you never stand up or get off the bench.
When Cook's shot left her hand, Coach's long time loyal assistant Willie Dutroy stood up.

He stood up right in front of Coach.

As the buzzer sounded Coach Dutroy seemed to lift off the floor.

All 255 pounds of him seemed to lift off the ground like a Macy's Day Parade balloon. The Warrior players on the bench sprinted to center court for a victory dog pile. The dam broke! Most of Empire's student cheering section also flooded the court. Although what seemed like the entire community of Empire had turned out for the game, it still only seemed to take up a minute section of the Coliseum. Now, however, it became a Sierra mountain avalanche. And it buried the court.

Coach Peterson was told later that Cook's shot was so true it barely moved the net, and fans from the upper deck couldn't even tell if it had gone in. The Empire High Warriors had not done the impossible, but they had succeeded in doing the highly improbable.

They had won the Division I California State Championship.

Swish happened!

Coach Peterson found himself standing all alone in front of the Warrior bench.

He stood paralyzed, staring out at the bedlam at center court. Players were jumping all over each other. Fans were hoisting them onto their shoulders. The California Interscholastic Federation Officials were making a desperate plea for them to clear the floor for the awards ceremony.

Coach found himself laughing. He used a hand to wipe away some tears. Suddenly he turned toward the stands and looked up to where his wife and son were sitting. He had taken the time to locate them during pre-game warm-ups. He pushed his way through the abandoned bench chairs and began to climb the arena stairs two at a time.

Some fans were still making their way down the steps to the coliseum floor so Coach had to force his way through the ascending crowd. They all wore faces of jubilation and celebration as Coach pushed his way by them. They were surprised to see him. Amazed he was crying. Puzzled by his sense of desperation as he made his way toward his wife's seat.

Joanie Peterson was standing by her seat; in her arms she was holding their three year old son, Parker.

She was smiling and laughing as she received congratulations from friends, groups of parents, and school officials. She glanced down at the floor and caught sight of Coach, now two rows below her, climbing the steps. He ignored the congratulations and slaps on the back as he made his way toward her. She spotted the tears rolling down his face. It was always her opinion that he was much too emotional about a game, but now she shook her head as she smiled down at him. She had to forgive him for this one.

Now Parker spotted Dad approaching, and a look of concern immediately appeared on his face.

Parker's going to wonder why the tears. Come on Dad, settle down! What's he's going to think? Settle down, Pete. Settle down!

Sure enough. A worried look appeared on Parker's face and tears instantly began to well up in his eyes as he extended both arms toward Coach.

Parker was so beautiful.

People always were stopping Coach and Joanie in the market and commenting about what a cute little boy he was. And he was. He was startlingly handsome for someone his age. But the truth was, he was simply beautiful.

Angelic.

He had Coach's mischievous grin, and even a little of Coach's physique was beginning to appear. But his looks came from his mother.

Joanie Peterson's face was striking.

She hadn't lost any of the beauty she enjoyed all her life. Even though she would be turning forty in a month, she was a very beautiful woman. Of course her overall appearance had matured. But her natural beauty was still very much evident. And she didn't maintain her allure with aerobics and anorexia like so many other mid-life panicked mothers her age. Spending precious time chasing adolescence on a treadmill—then chasing to get home. She preserved her vitality by not accepting an attitude of cerebral dormancy and dependence. Joanie sustained her beauty with family passion, responsibility and a reverence regarding relationships.

Parker had been blessed with Joanie's beauty.

Coach gathered them into his arms. For Coach the best feeling in the world was to squeeze Parker.

Joanie squeezed too.

"Congratulations Coach," she said.

"I love you, Joanie, and I love you, too, Parker," Coach said as he continued to hold them.

Coach leaned back and looked at Joanie now. He could see the pride and the love she had for her family.

Unlike Coach, Joanie did not wear her emotions on her sleeve. Sometimes it seemed like Coach had to beg for her approval. He grew frustrated sometimes, and he ached for signs of her affection.

But the bottom line was, Joanie was a wonderful mother. And a very devoted wife.

Their little family of Parker and Michelle, who was Joanie's daughter from a previous marriage, were the center of both Coach's and Joanie's universe.

Joanie's devotion to her family and her loyalty to Coach were never in question.

"We're champions, Parker!" Coach proclaimed.

"Champions, Dad," Parker responded.

"That's right, best buddy. Lets go get our picture taken." Coach leaned over and kissed Joanie. "Where's Michelle sitting?"

"Above us a few rows, " Joanie said as she let go of Parker and pointed to where Michelle sat.

Coach looked up to see Michelle standing and talking with her friends. She happened to be looking down at the three of them. Coach smiled up at her and waved. He gave her a thumbs up. She smiled and nonchalantly waved back. Even at her age you had to be cool around your friends.

Coach turned back to Joanie. "Honey, we'll be right back."

He lifted Parker up on his shoulders and headed back down to the arena floor.

Fans were beginning to return to their seats, and the CIF officials were starting to gain some order on the court.

The Warriors were lining up for their Championship photo. As Coach made his way down the aisle, he could see the players and Coach Dutroy searching the stands for him.

For over twenty years he had attended the State Championship game and dreamt about the possibilities. At times it seemed so distant, so remote, so unlikely. Too many obstacles. Especially for public schools these days. They didn't have the luxury of being able to recruit like the private schools. It had become a rarity for any public school to win a state championship in one of the five divisions in the state of California.

But Coach Peterson had always been a prisoner of hope.

Now he made his way down the isle to the arena floor with Parker on his shoulders.

It was a coronation.

Let it begin.

The Empire High Warriors were about to receive their crown as the California Girls Division I State Champions.

CHAPTER TWO

FEBRUARY 23, 2004

MONDAY MORNING

Coach was back in his study at dawn.

It had been almost three months. Hard to believe. Three months.

Joanie, Coach's wife, had a major blow up the night before. Yelling. Crying. Threatening. Threatening to call a doctor. Mental Health. He needed help. She needed help. Help in dealing with his behavior.

The depression.

It had been there for quite some time. Years maybe. She had recognized the symptoms years ago. But now? For Joanie it had grown into something that was now unbearable. Merciless.

Coach had just spent a month back in Wisconsin burying his father. When he returned, weeks went by and he rarely got out of his bathrobe. He never left the house. No gardening. No cooking. No chores at all. He even refused to walk down to the mailbox and retrieve the mail and morning newspaper.

He slept most of the day.

When he was awake he spent his time sitting on the couch staring at the TV. CNN. ESPN. Or he sat out on the back deck and smoked cigars, engulfed in some kind of stupor. Joanie despised smoking, and Coach was used to keeping it secret, always being very discreet. But now he didn't seem to care,

and her animated objections were ignored, her protests un-
heeded.

He even considered just staying in Wisconsin. Perma-
nently. He had absolutely no desire to return home to his wife.

*It's over. Dead. Why bother? There's nothing left. Can't be saved.
It's dead. My father. My life. Pretty much dead.*

It was his mother who finally persuaded him to go home.
More like demanded it.
And even though his mother was suffering, grieving, over
the loss of her husband of some sixty years, she still somehow
managed to convince him that Joanie still cared. That deep
down inside she needed him. That she still loved him.

Coach didn't buy all of it. Although minute, there was still
a part of him, alive enough, that believed in doing the responsible thing. And in spite of the tragedy, in spite of all the pain
and anguish that he felt liable for, he had to return. Return. And
continue to live with the constant, and immeasurable humiliation.
There was no escape. No parole.
He returned home to Northern California.

*How much more guilt could one man possess? When it comes to
collecting guilt, I'm the champ. Numero uno. Guinness Book of
Records. Thanks Mom. Didn't think there was room for anymore guilt.
Thought maybe my father's death finally had topped it off. I'm tired of
"doing the right thing" you know. Who cares? Anyone care?*

In all the years Joanie and Coach had been together, she
could count on one hand the number of times she left for work
and Coach was still in bed. When he was still teaching and
coaching basketball at the high school, he left for school before
she even got up. And since his retirement two years ago, he was
still always up at dawn and working in his study when she left.

But since his return from Wisconsin, he was always in bed when she left. And when she returned home late in the afternoon, he would be up but still dressed in his pajamas and bathrobe.

She was beginning to think his father's death had finally pushed him over the edge. He was slipping away. Slipping away for good.

Coach knew it too. Something was definitely wrong. He knew he had all the symptoms. A classic case. He was depressed. And he felt powerless to do anything about it.

Will I snap out of it? I'm not in any physical pain. I'm just tired. Very tired. A little more rest. I'll be fine with a little more rest. My father just passed away. I just need some time. Do I need help? A lifelong addiction of alcohol. And now this. Is this how it's going to end? Joanie ships me off to some mental hospital? Can she do that?

To Coach, it seemed like it took his entire lifetime before he realized what an incredible man his father was. Even more so now, in light of his own struggle to cope. Questions now abounded for him. Had he taken enough time to express his interest, his admiration and his love for his father? Had he managed to convey that before his father passed away? Or was he too caught up in his own life?

Too far away.

Too much distance. Too depressed.

He realized now that his father was an extraordinary man. Recognized now that he was part of an extraordinary generation.

And now he was gone.

Sorry bucko! Too late.

He now saw his father so differently. Characteristics that he once saw as weaknesses he now saw as attributes. His father was uncomplicated, undemanding, and humble. A modest individual who was devoted entirely to his wife and family for over sixty years. A man who had lived through the Great Depression. Fought and was wounded in World War II. A mailman. He got up and went to work at the same job for over forty years and never complained once.

He had a family. Enough to eat. Two weeks in the summer to go fishing. And one week in the fall to go deer hunting.

And for his father, it was enough.

He prayed every night. Not for more. Not for a better life. Instead he thanked the good Lord for what he had. And he asked God not to take it away.

The good with the bad. That was part of life. Sometimes life was tough, sometimes it was painful, sometimes it was unfair. It was all part of living, and he was grateful for that.

He never once considered trading the latest whatever for the beauty of a sunrise and a fishing pole.

And when his only son left home and moved two thousand miles away, he quietly accepted that too. That was part of life.

Be thankful.

Keep the faith.

For so long Coach never understood his father. He himself needed so much more.

Now Coach couldn't help feeling that the criticism of his father's values that he rendered so brutally during his rebellious college years hadn't been amended and reconciled enough. Back then he had openly scoffed at his father's work ethic. His faith. His conservatism. He had openly wondered, wasn't there more to life?

The 60s! Great stuff! Your ideals. Your opinions. There had to be more to life? Work all your life? For what? How can you be so satisfied with what you are? With what you have? Don't you want more? There has to be more! What a fool you were. What exactly were you thinking? Have another doobie.

But there wasn't more to life, and there didn't need to be. Coach had been blessed with a loving, hard-working, faithful father, and now he couldn't help feeling like it took him too long to realize it. And now he couldn't subdue the guilt. The overwhelming regret.

More shame. More remorse.

Eighty-one years old. And now he's gone. Too late now! You blew another one! You gave him two weeks these past few summers. Big deal! And some of those you chose to play golf with your buddies instead of fishing with your dad. Good job, Pete!

How can I go on? How can I ever capture the wonder, and the grace my father found in life? What's the use? I'm not strong enough. I'm tired of trying. Tired of living. I've had enough.

The truth, of course, was that Coach's feelings were totally unfounded. Erroneous. Delusional. Part of the depression. More self-pity. His father loved him deeply. There wasn't a father the world over that was prouder of his son. Always was. Always has been.

Living wasn't very important to Coach this morning, but he had risen with the sun and tried to reinstitute his routine and go about his normal daily rituals, the ones he was used to performing before returning from Wisconsin. Try to regain some normalcy in his life.

Have to get up. For Joanie. For Joanie. Fourth quarter. Push yourself. Turn on the computer. Check the mail. Check the e-mail. Sort magazines. Find the newspapers. See how the Lady Warriors are doing. Have some coffee. Fry some eggs. Take out the garbage. Watch SportsCenter. Maybe write some letters. Call Mom. It's raining. Used to love being a home body on rainy days.

Push yourself!

Push yourself!

Coach was firing up the computer when the commentator on SportsCenter began talking about the Western Pacific University Men's Basketball team. They were still undefeated in the

PAC-12. They only had two losses on the year, and they were a possible top seed in the upcoming NCAA Tournament. The tournament was just weeks away.

WPU was led by a nineteen year old wonder kid. A 6'4" point guard averaging a double-double as a sophomore. He was the PAC-12 leader in assists and steals. The highlights impressed Coach. Lester Travis. The name sounded familiar.

Great vision. Great passer. Unselfish. Looked to pass instead of score. Team leader. Floor general. Very competitive. And confident, but not too flashy.

Reminded Coach of one of his all time favorite point guards, John Stockton. Only this kid was taller, faster, and even more athletic.

Joanie came into say good-bye. Finding him in his study gave her a sense of relief, and she leaned over and kissed him on top of the head. Coach was back into his customary routine. She was feeling a whole lot safer. "Maybe he would be all right," she thought. Maybe she could start thinking about retiring herself. Last night the prospect of retiring terrified her.

"Go to the store, Pete. We're out of everything. You're in charge of dinner. I've got a late meeting. Don't even care if you get some steaks or want to throw some of those bratwurst things on the grill. See you at five-thirty, maybe six. Love you."

It didn't take much attention from Joanie to make Coach happy. An "I love you" from Joanie went a long way.

Today will be a good day.
No more crazy.
No more depression.

Joanie had piled up stacks of his unopened mail and weeks of magazines on his desk.

He decided the first thing he needed to do today was to sort
it all out. Clean house.

On the top of the stack of magazines was the latest *Sports
Illustrated*. On the cover was a picture of the WPU point guard,
Lester Travis. He was pictured on a beach holding a surf board.

The caption read, "WESTERN PACIFIC CATCHES A
WAVE."

Coach opened to the feature article and read.

Rich kid. Crosswoods High School-Los Angeles. State
Champs two years ago. Now Coach remembered where he had
heard the name. Beat St. Ignacious of San Francisco for the
Championship. All five starters got Division I scholarships.

Coach read on.

He was the son of a big time movie producer, Edward
Travis. Edward Travis had recently started a multi-million dol-
lar partnership with the rich and famous actor, Gregory Stone.
Made lots of movies. Made lots of money.

His kid, Lester Travis, had everything growing up in
Santa Monica. Big mansion. Attendants. Dad had a private jet.
Took him everywhere. By the time he was a teenager, he had
been around the world. Spent time on exotic movie sets. Af-
rica. Asia. South America. He grew up coddled by famous
actors and actresses. Met famous athletes. Sat in his dad's
private box at the Forum and the Staples Center and watched
the Lakers.

All the time he kept his own hoop dreams alive. Carried his
ball around wherever he went.

In high school the kid had his own sports car. He would
drive it down to the harshest asphalt courts in Los Angeles and
play pick-up basketball. Never backed down from anyone.
Earned him a lot of respect by some tough kids in some tough
neighborhoods. He was never aware of the fact that his father
was hiring body guards to secretly keep an eye on him.

He attended the best camps. Received private instruction from retired NBA Lakers. Magic Johnson, Kareem Abdul-Jabbar and James Worthy were mentioned.

His summer AAU teams were almost totally funded by his father. They had the finest equipment. The latest uniforms. They stayed in the best hotels. A Nike sponsorship picked up any loose ends.

It wasn't hard for his father and his AAU coach to hand pick the team. Word got around. They had the best players from all over the West Coast. Sometimes they stayed at the Travis Mansion between summer tournaments.

They were not only one of the best summer teams on the West Coast, but one of the best teams in the country. Winning tournaments in Vegas, Orlando, Chicago, and Philadelphia.

Dad also made sure Lester was surrounded by talent in high school too. There were no limits to district movement in California anymore. Coach knew the state's interscholastic athletic governing body had thrown up its hands a long time ago. Lester's high school teams were loaded. Filled with transfers from other school districts. Travis started on the varsity as a freshman.

When it came time to go to college, he chose his father's alma mater. His father was a graduate from Western Pacific. WPU was a small expensive private university located on the Southern California coast below Los Angeles and north of San Diego. It had one of best film schools in the country, now made even more famous by the fact that Edward Travis was a graduate.

When Lester was a senior in high school, Western Pacific had hired a new head coach by the name of Jeff Schmidt. He was a former assistant under Rick Majerus at Utah. He had spent two years as head coach at Pepperdine where he was an instant success. He then was lured away to a floundering WPU program. Some say by the help of Travis and some other important, and wealthy alumni.

In two years at WPU, Schmidt had managed to recruit some of the best young talent in the country. The article went on to say that they were young, but definitely talented enough to make a serious run at the National Championship.

Coach was studying the pictures.

Good looking kid. Short hair. Sideburns. Chiseled. Didn't have the tattoos like most of the players these days. No earrings either. Familiar looking. Can't remember seeing him play in high school.

Coach didn't watch as many college games as he used to.

He stared at one particular photo a long time. It showed Lester standing by his famous father in their own private gym.

Didn't look much like his father. Built different. Lester was much taller. Familiar. Very familiar.

Apprehension. Anxiety. Then terror!

A panic attack!

It's the player in my dream! The one in the locker room of my old high school. The one in my nightmare. It can't be. That's absurd. That's crazy. I am losing it. It can't be! I swear! It is! It is!

It's Parker!

CHAPTER THREE

FEBRUARY 11, 1993

THURSDAY NIGHT

NORTH GYM

"Defense wins games. Rebounding wins championships. How many times do I have to remind you people of that?"

Coach Peterson almost added, "What a bunch of crap," out loud, but he kept that to himself.

To Coach it was putting the ball in the basket that really mattered. It was offense that won games. All that other stuff was just a way to get players to practice the less glamorous parts of the game. Of course defense and rebounding were important, but if you couldn't score. . . .

"How many missed lay-ups? Five? Six? Three for nine from the free-throw line? We've got to make these things! We've got to concentrate! This team has no business being on the same floor with you guys!"

Coach was using one of his time-outs four minutes before halftime.

The fact that he was using it this close to halftime showed his level of frustration with the way the Warriors were playing. Let alone the fact that he had just said something so stupid.

Make your shots. Like a player needs to be reminded of that?

To Coach those were the kind of things that always signaled inexperience. They signaled, well, bad coaching.

He used a time-out, but he hadn't given the players anything they could use to get back in the game. No defensive or offensive adjustment. They didn't need a rest. They didn't need to break the other team's momentum. And they certainly didn't need to be reminded to make their shots.

The fact was, his team wasn't playing with any intensity.

They were not playing hard.

And Coach Peterson knew it was a reflection on his coaching.

It used to be his strength. His edge.

His sense of desperation and urgency were always contagious.

Coach could always motivate. His own life was a model for motivation.

He sweat with his players. He sweat with them in practice, and he sweat with them in games. His preparation and teaching were always meticulous and organized. Now it was sloppy. Impatient. Unstructured.

He had lost his confidence.

He had lost his desire. The hunger.

Coach Dutroy had filled in some of the void. He always put together a tough defense for the Warriors. Tough man to man. Pressure defense. Pressure on the ball. Full court press.

But now Willie had to take more responsibility for teaching the offense. And other areas of the program required more of his attention as well. Willie had to be vigilante, constantly reminding Coach of things they had to do. Things that needed to be done. Preparation that had been neglected. Things Coach had overlooked. Things that Coach had never before neglected or failed to ignore.

Coach Dutroy was a great coach. But he wasn't the organizer, the motivator or the promoter that Coach was. When it came to promotion, there was no one better than Coach. He was the P.T. Barnum of high school girl's basketball, not only in Gold County, but in Northern California.

The Lady Warriors were on radio and cable TV.

They sold programs, posters, and athletic apparel. The Booster Club he had started raised annually over twenty thousand. It bought uniforms, travel equipment, warm-ups, and shoes for the Frosh, JV, and Varsity. It also allowed the Varsity to travel to out of state tournaments. The Warriors had traveled to San Antonio, Anchorage, Las Vegas, San Diego, Wyoming and Ohio.

Now the team hadn't traveled out of state for five years.

His summer camps had always been filled.

He had to turn kids away most years. The last two summers the numbers were down. Way down. And interest was continuing to decline.

It's me. People think I'm a freak. Ever since . . .

Young female athletes in the gold country used to grow up dreaming of becoming a Lady Warrior Basketball Player. All Coach had to do was get them to a game. He knew about every prospect in the county and would invite them to a game or have their youth league team play at halftime. He knew they would feel the excitement, witness it first hand, and they would get hooked.

So many sports were year-round now. You had to compete with the other programs for committed athletes. And Coach was used to getting the cream of the crop. To insure that, however, you had to keep winning. It was all predicated on success.

Coach had become an icon. Won numerous championships. Won state. Was elected California Coach of the Year.

But he knew the trouble with being an icon is that eventually they want to put you on a shelf and worship you from a distance.

Last year was only the second year in Coach's thirteen seasons as the Warrior's Head Coach that they didn't make the playoffs. And they were in the same position they were in at this time last year.

They had to win their last three games to guarantee a playoff spot.

Two wins might get it, if they got a little help from someone else. But it would still mean having to play on the road in the first round.

Twice in Coach's tenure the Warriors were on the road in the first round, and twice they failed to advance.

Although the community was sympathetic toward Coach, sympathetic about the family tragedy, he knew there were a lot of fan rumblings. He heard the rumors.

They think it's time for me to get out. Find someone else to drive the band wagon. The band wagon that I built. After all it's their daughters' turn. A chance for their scholarships. And they think they're not getting the exposure that requires. When you win, the players get the credit. But when you lose, no matter what the circumstances, the coach always gets the blame.

Coach won his three hundredth game this season.

That was an average of just over twenty-three wins a season. It was a phenomenal record. But it was a win total padded by teams from earlier years. Teams that won thirty or more games. This was another season. They would only win twenty by getting deep into the playoffs. Some programs would kill for a single twenty win season. But the Warriors had high standards. The bar was set high and the fans expected them to consistently get over it.

Coach knew that coaching wasn't just what have you done for me lately, it was what have you done for me today?

There were rumors that the Athletic Director Michael Kelly was going to get the school board to approve naming the old North Gym after him. To Kelly, Coach deserved it. But there still were concerns by the board.

"What about the drinking?"

"And the thing with his son. What about the thing with his son?"

What have you done for me today?

Coach had heard those rumors too. Like so many others, they blamed him.

He actually had dreamed of the old gym wearing his name someday. Dreams of Parker being a student at Empire while his dad was a popular and successful coach. He had wanted to stay in coaching long enough so Parker would grow up knowing his dad as a coach. He wanted Parker tagging along with him to practice. Shooting around on a side basket, and maybe when he was a little older, running drills with the Warriors. Even scrimmaging with them.

Parker would have grown up with the game. And he would have been a great player. The son of a winning coach. A point guard. Floor leader. A coach on the floor.

The recruiters would be breaking down the door. He would maybe get a chance to meet the coaches he himself admired and studied. The coaches who designed the material he ran.

Together they would have picked the school he would attend and the coach he would play for.

Now Coach figured Kelly was getting pressure from fans, and maybe even the school administration, to figure out a way to ease out the "old guy."

Kelly and Coach had become very close over the years. Kelly was a long time assistant varsity football coach.

Coaching was in their blood.

It was what they essentially were.

They both understood what it was like to be in the ring with the bulls.

They had worked together a long time and confronted many problems together. Now Coach figured that even his good friend thought it might be time to hang it up. Time to start thinking about retiring.

It had to be hard for Kelly.

He had two sons himself. Parker and Kelly's boys went to the same pre-school. They played together.

As Kelly's boys grew older they accompanied him to games and practices, and you could see how proud he was of them. How proud he was of the way they looked up to him.

Because of that he could feel Coach's pain almost more than anyone else.

To use the gym naming as a way to get his friend out of coaching was ugly. Gut wrenching. Kelly felt that Coach Peterson had to leave on his own terms when he was ready. But there was the pressure. And he didn't want him to stay around too long. Become a joke. A laughing stock. Someone to take pity on. A parody of himself.

Coach would be forty-nine this summer.

He used to be so proud of the fact that people were surprised at his age. He looked ten, even fifteen years younger than he really was. Five years ago he was still playing and playing well. Still running suicides with his teams.

Now he could barely get out of bed.

He was heavy and out of shape. The bike tires on his mountain bike were flat. They had been for quite some time.

He still had a full head of hair, but it was graying and unkempt. He hadn't purchased a new piece of clothing in five years.

It was almost impossible for Coach to be the least bit social. He was unfriendly and his impoliteness toward his colleagues grew. He avoided coffee and donuts before teachers' meetings. Sometimes he skipped the meetings altogether. Didn't play in the annual faculty golf tournament. He didn't go to coaching clinics anymore.

His classroom was once noisy and active.

Students had worked together on projects. Students had been required to do oral presentations and participate in simulations.

Players and students used to hang around between classes and eat their lunch in his room. Coach was not the most innovative teacher or the most knowledgeable, but he connected. He touched every student he came in contact with. He was friendly. He told stories. He was a comedian.

His greatest attribute as a teacher was the fact that kids knew he genuinely cared about them. Cared about each and everyone of them. He was comfortable around kids, and they were comfortable around him. They teased him, and he teased them back. There was not a day he wasn't excited about getting up and going to school. He never considered teaching a job. He never considered it work. It was a privilege. It was a hobby.

However, in these last few years his classes had grown quiet.

Students sat in rows. He became more of a disciplinarian. Less tolerant. Disliked movement. Disliked noise. He now wrote more discipline referrals than most of the other teachers. Some days his tolerance level was zero, and he would blow up over minor infractions.

Kids called him "Xerox" as they plodded through units of worksheets.

His classrooms still had bulletin boards full of articles and pictures of student achievement, but none of them were recent. The walls were still covered with framed team photos, but they were crooked and dusty.

Coach had become just like his classroom.

Distant and uncaring.

He could hardly be blamed for being distracted and depressed.

For the last five years he spent hours upon hours sitting at his computer. Searching the internet for information was his morning routine. He was in constant contact with the National Center for Missing and Exploited Children in Arlington, Virginia. He was working with the National Children's Locate Center. He was familiar with all the missing children in the country.

He knew their names.

Their faces.

He had contact with their parents, sometimes speaking to them on the phone. He did, however, resist ever meeting with them or going to a support group.

He wasn't a joiner.

Many of the parents dealt with their loss by becoming crusaders. But Coach felt like their only interest was finding their own son or daughter. Besides most of them were kidnapped by parents in custody battles. They would eventually find their child and be reunited. The police knew exactly who did it and it was just a matter of time before they caught up with them. There were thousands and thousands of those cases every year.

Coach, on the other hand, felt his situation was so much different, Parker was part of a small, unique percentage.

His percentage disappeared completely without a trace. Probably victims of serials. They were never found. And if they were, it was usually a decaying body, or bones. And the dental records were the only thing that reunited the parents with their child.

There were days he spent at the Sacramento malls.

At first he would find an excuse.

Tell Joanie he needed to go to Sacramento for one reason or another. Sometimes he would be so distraught he would just go. Not really caring what Joanie thought.

He would just drive in silence. No radio. Music was too agonizing now.

He would park in different places around the mall and sit. Watching. Staring at the people walking by.

Sometimes he would get out and walk. Stopping to sit outside Footlocker. He would sit there for hours, studying every face that came by.

Was it him? How about her? If I could just find them they could be made to talk. They would be made to confess. No matter what had happened I would find out. Because that's the worst part. The not knowing. It's too painful to think Parker is. . . . But wouldn't that be better than the not knowing?

Coach couldn't help but keep remembering the last Halloween with Parker. Right after he turned three. Every night when he was putting Parker to bed, Parker would ask him, "Dad, are there really monsters?"

"No, Parker. This Halloween thing is all make-believe. There really aren't monsters."

But Coach was wrong. Coach had lied.

There really were monsters.

Now Coach and Joanie's marriage had all but disappeared.

They didn't sit on the couch together and read the papers anymore. They didn't watch the news together. They didn't rent movies. Or go to movies. They stopped going out to dinner. Things they did on a regular basis together slowly disappeared.

They rarely even spoke to each other. They didn't go to bed together at the same time. And they never got up together.

Coach missed Joanie.

He missed everything they once had. He especially missed her friendship. She was his best friend. He missed her so badly the pain was almost as great as losing Parker.

Joanie didn't openly blame Coach.

That would have been too cruel. After all, he blamed himself. And that was more torture than anyone should have to bear. She just tolerated him.

Their life had been Michelle and Parker. Now Michelle had gone off to college in Stockton to follow in her mom's footsteps as a speech therapist.

The house was empty.

And so were they.

On Sundays Coach went to church by himself.

Even before Parker disappeared, he was a regular. He was baptized and raised a Lutheran back in Wisconsin, and he continued worshipping in California as a Lutheran. Joanie, on the other hand, was raised a Mormon and had stopped going to church years before they had met. Coach was not what you would say devout in his commitment to working within the church, but he rarely missed a Sunday service. His relationship with God was strained to say the least. To still be a believer after Parker's disappearance was, in a sense, remarkable.

What kind of God would allow something like this to happen? How can you give yourself up to a higher power that would let something like this happen? I'm not a bad person. Never hurt anyone. I was faithful. I was honest. I'm a believer. I would rather have my own life taken away. A test in faith? Anything. Anything but this.

But Coach knew he needed God.

Needed God more than ever. Without God he would be incapable of kindness. Incapable of love. He would be discouraged, cruel and suicidal. Without God his grief would be too unbearable.

With God he still had some hope.

Hope.

Yvonne Wallace rebounded a missed Warrior shot, put it in, and got fouled. If she makes the free-throw the Warriors would be within seven with three and a half minutes to go.

Coach called another time-out.

"Match-up on the free-throw. When Yvonne knocks down the free-throw, trap the first pass. Everyone rotates. The pass back to the inbounder is the one we want. Let's go! Lots of time left. No stupid fouls."

Coach felt the tingle. Slight. But it was there.

He had a flash of optimism.

Sure enough, the free-throw was good. The Warriors trapped the unsuspecting guard, and she tried to pass back to the post who inbounded it. Meagan Witt intercepted it under the Warrior basket and forced up a quick shot.

She missed it.

But she got her own rebound. She pivoted and kicked it out to the Warrior point guard, Carrie Brooks, who had sprinted back to the top of the key. She caught it as she jump stopped behind the arc.

Fired.

Net.

The Warriors were now within four points and in their jump rotate press.

The Wolf Creek Wolves were panicking.

Their coach was frantically trying to call a time-out, but the Warrior crowd was into it now, and his players didn't hear him. They threw it away at half court.

He got his time-out.

But it was the Warriors' ball.

"Let's run our Hoosier special side inbound play guys. Set good screens. Before the ball is inbounded check to see who you are screening. And then nail 'em!"

The play was a triple screen or picket fence as it's sometimes called. Brooks had just hit a three, and Coach hoped she had another one in her.

"Carrie, if they get help or switch, look for your wings. Sara Rick. Or Carley Fitzhugh. Someone will be open."

The team was excited. They looked confident. Coach knew they were starting to feel it. And so was he.

Brooks caught the pass, but her defender had fought through the screen. No shot. But Sara Rick's man came to help. Brooks quickly fired a pass to her.

She drilled it.

Warriors within one!

Now the Wolves were playing not to lose and were moving the ball nervously up the court. It was close to a minute left. The shot clock was down to six seconds, and they threw up a bad shot.

Wallace rebounded.

Outlet to Brooks.

Long pass to Fitzhugh.

Layup.

And she was fouled!

The free-throw was good. The Warriors had the lead now, and were in control.

The Wolves would miss again and begin to foul intentionally.

Warriors win going away.

Coach felt alive.

He was proud of his team. They had played hard at the end. Executed.

It was short and fleeting, but for an instant he was his old self. Felt like he still had it. He gazed up into the stands, behind the bench where most of the parents sat, and he saw happy faces. Cheering faces.

He looked at the area in the bleachers where his family used to sit. Joanie, Parker, and Michelle.

Empty.

Very rarely did anyone ever sit in that particular spot. Even now. It was like it was still off limits. Everyone knew not to sit there. Those seats are reserved! That's the spot where Coach's wife sits. Coach's family.

But Joanie hadn't been to a game in the last five years.

He wished she were there tonight. It would have felt like old times.

Parker would have been eight now. Already becoming a hot blooded Peterson. That competitiveness beginning to burn. Upset when the Warriors lost. Happy when they won.

He would have been proud of his pop tonight.

The fans headed home. Coach Dutroy was putting the equipment away and was excitedly talking about their chances of making the playoffs. Maybe making a run. Getting some playoff experience for the underclassmen. This was a young team, and the experience would be valuable. Next year they could be a contender.

Coach hadn't looked ahead for a long time. Not in a positive light. Tomorrow's were just more of the same.

Guilt.

Shame.

Disgrace.

But tonight's win did give him a lift.

Tonight was a little like old times. Willie suggested getting cigars, and Coach agreed. They drove down to the mini-mart and smoked them in the parking lot. They talked about the game. Reminisced. And made plans for the playoffs.

Coach eventually dropped Willie off back at his car in the school lot, and headed home.

A chilly rain began to fall.

Man it's getting cold. Might even turn to snow by morning.

Coach was enjoying the win. He felt good.

Should I feel guilty? Why? Is it wrong to feel alive again? Maybe Parker was still alive. Even if he wasn't he would be in heaven waiting for me. Either way, wasn't he alive? Couldn't I then be alive too? Couldn't I feel good for awhile? Even be happy again, if just for a while? The good Lord was a God of the living. Of everlasting life.

He decided to try harder.

CHAPTER FOUR

FEBRUARY 19, 1998

THURSDAY NIGHT

"Peterson, you are such a gunner!"

Pete wasn't sure which Raider the comment came from.

"I was never so open in my whole life! The ref should have called me for a three-second violation every time down the floor. I think he felt sorry for me. I was underneath the hoop waving my arms, you asshole." Pete recognized that one. The comment came from his best friend Barry, nicknamed Chico.

"Thirty-six points! Peterson, you were on fire!"

That comment came from one of many teammates who were now all beginning to arrive in the locker room.

"Raiders rule!"

"We are the Champions!"

They were pushing each other, laughing, singing, and slapping hands. The Raiders had just beaten the Clintonville Truckers to clinch the Mid-Eastern Conference Championship.

"Pete" Peterson had just put on a clinic.

Fifteen for 22 from the field and a perfect 6 for 6 from the line.

All of Pete's closest friends and teammates were now in the locker room. Besides Chico there was Rugs, Saco, Mosey, Denny B, Laeszo, Rudy, Lucky, Guy Bear, and Ziffel.

In Wisconsin, everyone had a nickname. Tradition.

It was Washington High's first ever basketball championship.

A dream season.

They were undefeated in league and had beaten Clintonville for the second time giving the Truckers their only two losses on the season.

Payback! Revenge!

Last year a bitter overtime loss to the Truckers cost them the Championship. Now they had clinched the league championship with one game remaining.

"Peterson!" It was Coach Haege yelling now. His arrival to the locker room brought the Raiders around him into a semicircle.

"You can't dribble or pass worth a shit. But you sure can shoot. Every time you go to put the ball on the floor, I about crap a crooked nail. But I'm going to give you a big kiss. Cuz Peterson, you deserve it." The huge Head Coach gave Pete a big bear hug, lifting him off the floor, and kissed him on top of the head. The rest of the team began to hoot and holler.

"Congratulations, boys!" Coach Haege now turned to address the whole team. "Now that's what I call defense, boys. Man, your defense was tighter then a bulls ass at fly time. You've worked hard, fellas. Very hard. You deserved to win this thing. I'm very proud of you. The school. The whole community. They're all proud of you. Now don't you all go nuts tonight and blow this thing. There is still a lot this team can accomplish. Next step is to win the section. And then go down state. We have a lot of work still ahead of us boys. We can do it. Now I don't want you guys to get carried away by this. Let's not stop here. Training rules are still in effect. I don't want to hear about anybody going out to Vic's and getting shit-faced. If I hear about it, so help me, you're a goner. That goes for everyone! Are you listening, Ziffel?"

All the boys laughed. Ziffel was known to stretch team rules on occasion. Vic's was a local beer bar located just outside the town limits. The establishment was a little lax when it came to checking ID's. Ziffel was practically a regular.

Pete was ecstatic.

The gym had been packed. Raucous. Standing room only. It seemed like the entire town was dressed up in purple and gold.

Two years ago Haege was hired as the Head Coach of the Washington High Raiders.

In just two years he had managed to turn the program around completely. And it was Pete's good fortune to be a part of it. The Raiders had lost a combined five games in those two years.

Haege was tough. Vulgar. Intimidating. Mean. Sometimes down-right cruel.

But he was more than just a demanding disciplinarian and uncompromising taskmaster. He was a gifted tactician. He was incredibly inspirational. A master motivator. He managed to challenge each and everyone of them to get better. Because of his unique ability, his players were more than willing to pay the price. And in return they received such a deep sense of pride, and a shared mutual respect, it would bond them all forever.

Pete had big games before.

But to have one with this much at stake was inconceivable. His boyhood dreams were all coming true. And then some. He was a high school star. And the chance of getting a scholarship to the University of Wisconsin in Madison was beginning to become a real possibility.

The admiration on the faces of the fans in the stands. The recognition by strangers around town It was all wonderful stuff. Heady stuff.

Sally LeClair, the prettiest girl in school, was his steady. She had moved from Lake Geneva the year before, and all the guys went for her. But she had become his girlfriend.

Her parents loved him too.

Her dad was the new local First Methodist Church Pastor, an ex-college basketball star himself, and he had become one of Pete's biggest fans.

And of course there was his own father who just couldn't hide the pride he had for his son. His father's approval meant more than all the other things put together.

Pete's father had to work so hard. Long hours. Besides a rural mail route that took him out on the road at 5 AM, he took other jobs sometimes working the night shift at a local factory just so the family could make ends meet, or have a little something extra. He was a man who had little time for anything else, wasn't overly emotional, didn't say all that much. But Pete just knew he was gaining his admiration.

His father was a very fine athlete in his own right and might have gone on to play college ball himself if the World War II hadn't come along. Pete knew that part of his success now was a result of trying to please his father. It drove him. It was the one thing he could do to show his appreciation. And knowing that to some degree he was accomplishing that was the greatest reward of all. By far and away worth all the sacrifice and hard work.

"Pete," It was Coach Haege again. "You are really learning how to play this game."

"You're playing hard, and you're playing under control. Very smart. You're leadership is one of the reasons we've accomplished what we have so far."

Only now it wasn't Coach Haege saying it.

It was him. Coach Peterson!
He was saying it!

He was speaking to a young teenage player who was sitting on a bench in front of his locker taking off his shoes. He didn't recognize him, but there was something very familiar about him.

"You were outstanding tonight, Parker," Coach Peterson said to the young athlete.

The kid stopped untying his shoes and looked up at the Coach.

"Dad. Are there monsters?"

Instantly Coach Peterson awoke!
His eyes were wide open and wet. He was breathing fast and perspiring. Clammy.

Jeez! Am I having a heart attack?

It was a new one.
A new nightmare.

It had taken one of his greatest moments, one of his proudest memories, and turned into a horrible dream. Just when he thought the bad memories had begun to subside, it came up with a new way of torturing him.

Ten years.
It was ten years now.

Great! A tenth year anniversary present.

Coach knew better than to try and go back to sleep. He stumbled out of bed and went to the bathroom. It was only four-thirty in the morning, but Coach knew it was hopeless to try and sleep after the dreams awoke him.

Today was the last game of the regular season.
The last home game. The last scheduled home game he would ever coach.
The Warriors had qualified for the play-offs and had a fine young team. Tami Collier, A.C. Pietrek, and Kassidy McCauley were all juniors. All starters. Very fast, and very athletic.
It would leave Coach Dutroy with a great returning team. A team that could possibly win the league and even the section championship.
It was tempting for Coach to return, but he was fifty-four now, getting close to calling it quits altogether. Retirement from

teaching was just around the corner. Starting next year he could qualify. No penalty. The California State Retirement System could begin paying him monthly.

It was time.

He had guided the Warriors for eighteen seasons. Won over four hundred games. Won eight Section Championships and a state title.

He had become a legacy in women's high school hoops in the state of California.

He had lasted twenty-six years as a head coach.

Twenty-six years in the days most high school coaches lasted an average of two or three. These days most got out as soon as they got their teaching tenure.

Times had changed, and most of the changes made it increasingly difficult to stay in coaching.

Besides the increasing time it took to run a top notch program, raising the money, driving the bus, doing all the scheduling, being the custodian of your gym, monitoring your players academics, taking CPR and first aid training, and a million other things, discipline was probably the biggest challenge.

Not only did the administration not want to deal with the discipline, neither did the parents.

It was a simple fact.

The only disciplinarians left out there were coaches.

Surprisingly, most of the kids wanted it. The discipline. Welcomed it.

They sought out sports for some semblance of structure in their lives. The team provided a sense of belonging, a sense of security. But when it came time to lay down the law and act on it, most coaches no longer had anybody to back them up.

Especially the parents, who basically didn't discipline their own children. Couldn't discipline them. And resented it when anyone else tried.

The parents not only thought they were qualified experts on coaching, they also had become experts on the educational system and consistently felt they knew what was best for their child. The continual criticism, constant faultfinding, and derogatory scrutinization by parents made it so much more difficult to teach young people anything. The truth was, kids hadn't changed so much over the years, but the parents sure had.

Combined with the lack of support from parents, salaries weren't keeping up with inflation. It didn't make sense to go to college for five years, considering the investment that took these days, and then get out and make what a teacher's starting salary. Those factors and more were leading to a massive shortage of qualified teachers all over the country.

Besides, the kids were witness to the disrespect their parents were dishing out about the state of education. They witnessed first hand their teacher's frustration with being underfunded and underpaid. "The building they work in is falling down, for gosh sakes! Nothing works! Look at the houses they live in, look at the cars they drive!" Their parents practically viewed them as nonprofessionals, and because of that, so did many of the students. Parents just didn't realize that a little positive reinforcement could work wonders for their child's education and their overall well-being.

While the overall life expectancy for teachers and coaches had become short, somehow Coach had survived.

Survived through perseverance. Survived out of necessity. He had to reinvent himself, time and time again, but he kept going.

These last five years when he decided to recommit himself, had been some of his most enjoyable and rewarding of all his years in coaching. It was some of his best work. And it brought back some of his feelings of self-worth.

Not just as a Coach, but as a teacher.

In these last few years some of the guilt had begun to subside. Coach felt that unconsciously Joanie still couldn't help blaming him for Parker. She probably blamed him for the loss of their relationship. However, there were actually short periods of reprieve. Their relationship? He did accept some responsibility for that. At least in part.

He found it pretty much impossible to be romantic or intimate. These last ten years there were just too many things that were left unsaid.

They basically began to live separate lives.

They shared a bed, at least a couple of hours a night. But the rest of the time they occupied different areas of the house. She had the living room and he had Michelle's old bedroom, which he had converted into a study. They came and went separately, briefly sharing each others schedule and then living a life that seemingly no longer included each other.

Their life was filled and fulfilled with work. They both still loved their work. Were dedicated. Believed in what they did made a difference for kids. But that passion and love was no longer shared for each other.

There was a void in their lives that neither could fill.

And that emptiness grew.

Coach made his way downstairs and began his morning routine, microwaving a cup of leftover coffee while a fresh pot brewed. He went to his study and switched on the computer. Checked the mail.

He turned on the study TV and used the remote to go back and forth between news and sports.

The safest place for Coach was his study. There he felt secure. Somewhat protected. Especially at this time of the morning. The memories followed him everywhere, but in his study, in his room, he felt less vulnerable, and he could let a little of the outside world in.

Retirement. I won't ever have to leave this room. Never venture out. I can live in here. Be safe. Grow old. Die. The dreams. The pain. Would go away. Wouldn't it?

Last night's nightmare gave him a glimpse of some of his old buddies. His old teammates, some of whom he hadn't seen in thirty years. Most of them were still alive. Lucky had died in Vietnam. Guy Bear drank himself to death. But most were still around living in the Midwest. Christmas cards still arrived from some of them. But for over the last ten years, most of the time they went unanswered.

He used to send them updates, articles and tapes, chronicling various milestones and achievements. State or Section Championships. Three hundredth, four hundredth, career wins.

But it became too difficult to share his life.

It even took a maximum effort to keep his parents informed about his life.

Coach wasn't even sure if his parents still read the articles or even could read them. Both his parents were in their late seventies and their health was deteriorating. Not a whole lot of mobility left. They primarily concentrated on taking care of each other, and they did a fantastic job of that. Most of their days they filled up with going to see doctors. They still had one of the greatest love affairs of all time. Had seen it all and stayed together through sickness and health, good times and bad. In four years they will have been married sixty years.

Without coaching maybe now he would have more time to rekindle some of those old relationships. Make new friends with old friends. Maybe take a trip and look up some old acquaintances. Spend more time back in Wisconsin with his sisters and his parents.

I'll make a list, a list of things to do now that I'll have more time. Prepare for retirement. Write letters. Send e-mails. Phone old friends.

An image returned from his latest nightmare. He saw the young player he was speaking to in the locker room.

The face. Was it my face? Sorta. But not really.

It was his face.
It was Parker's face!
Was it? How could that be? He was three.

Coach tried to recreate the images from his dream.

He had short dark hair. Not as dark as his, but darker than Joanie's. It was cut short. Short enough that it didn't need to be combed. He had bright brown eyes surrounded by long dark eyelashes and thick eyebrows. His skin was dark, almost green. And it made the color in his cheeks and lips stand out even more.

His face was perfect.

More than handsome. He was beautiful.

He was tall and chiseled. Not as stocky and Slavic like Coach. Parts of his face needed a shave, his chin, his upper lip, maybe his sideburns, but it didn't detract from his looks. This boy was a good looking kid. Radiant. Almost feminine.

It wasn't his own image he saw.

It was more like Joanie's.

When Coach was in college, like everyone around his age, he was obsessed with trying to explain the universe.

Find the meaning of life.

And like everyone else at that time, his quest took him down many paths.

He read many different books. Books by Carlos Castaneda, Bubba Ram Dass. Books about Zen Buddhism. He took LSD. Tried transcendental meditation.

But now he was a Christian.

His faith allowed him to accept things as unexplainable. He accepted the fact that something's were beyond his understanding. Something's remain a mystery. Should remain a mystery.

Strange and unexplainable things do happen. Visions. Was my dream one of them?

Was it Parker?
Was he alive? Do you age in heaven?

It was a vision.

Or was it?

CHAPTER FIVE

JUNE 8, 2002

SATURDAY MORNING

> "May God bless and keep you always,
> And your wishes all come true,
> And may you always do for others,
> And let others do for you."

> "May you build a ladder to the stars,
> And climb on every rung,
> And may you stay, forever young."

When the principal asked Coach to speak at graduation, in honor of his retirement and his lengthy tenure at Empire High School, she didn't know he was going to get a Bob Dylan impersonator.

Coach hadn't picked up a guitar since college. And even then he never got past C-D-G. Now he was strumming away and using his best weeping Dylan wail.

I'm way too nervous to pull this off. This is crazy. Way too out of the ordinary. What was I thinking? A folk song for a graduation speech! Hello! Yeah. Who cares anyway? This is it! You're out of here!

> "Forever young, forever young,
> May you stay, forever young"

46

After the first verse, he gradually starting to accumulate a little more confidence. Exhibit more conviction. With his inhibitions evaporating he began to pump the volume even more.

Barry, his high school best friend, better known as Chico, had an older brother named Nick. Nick was a retired forester who lived up in Shasta and now spent his time playing in a country band. He was on stage with Coach helping him out with his graduation speech. Nick's expertise was an essential addition to Coach's wild rendition of Bob Dylan's song, "Forever Young."

Even Nick, however, had never played in front of this many people before. There were five, maybe, six thousand people in the Empire High Football Stadium.

The five hundred plus graduates sat in chairs facing the stage in the middle of the field.

They stared up at the crazy old man singing his heart out to one of his favorite old songs. Most had never heard of Bob Dylan, unless maybe as freshman if they had "Mr. Peterson" for a teacher. Then they probably remember him expounding on the fact that Dylan was not just a great song writer, but the greatest poet of the last century.

> "May you grow up to be righteous,
> May you grow up to be true,
> May you always know the truth,
> And see the light surrounding you.
> May you always be courageous,
> Stand upright and be strong,
> And may you stay, forever young."

The truth was that most of the grads didn't even know who Coach was.

He had been out of coaching for four years, so he was out of the community limelight. It doesn't take very long before they forget about you. His name could no longer be found in the local sports pages. His interviews were no longer heard on the radio.

There out there wondering who I am. How soon they forget. Gone, and forgotten. Only to be left a legend in his own mind! Eee-hah!

Over the last few years Coach taught primarily freshman classes. Less than a hundred new students a year. And for one reason or another, a certain percentage of those didn't even make it to graduation. He really didn't get to know that many students in a school this size anymore. And without basketball...

"Who is this guy?"

"Was this the guy they named the old gym after?"

"The old gym that's used for dance classes?"

"He was a dance teacher?"

"This is our graduation speech?"

"Forever young, forever young,
May you stay, forever young."

Coach used to love being a clown.

He used to love opportunities to get silly, get crazy, be the comedian. And he was good at it. He could bring down the house at faculty meeting or at lunch in the teachers' lounge. He especially looked for opportunities when he thought things were getting too negative or people were taking themselves much too seriously like union meetings or when the yearly news would arrive down from the hill where the district office stood...

"Sorry guys, no raise again this year. Oh, and your department budgets are getting cut again."

There were times he got a little carried away. Offended some people. But most of the time he was successful in getting people to laugh at themselves.

Since Parker, most of his talent for levity had disappeared. But some evidence of that crazy, silly, singing comedian actually began to reappear these last few years. A little bit here. A little bit there. His sense of humor had been lost far too long. What was it? Ten years? Twelve? Fourteen?

The power of laughter was an important part of who he was. Or at least, what he used to be.

This was, by far an away, his most effective quality when it came to teaching.

Coach was wired to make students laugh. His energy, his ability to make his students laugh was the foundation of his relationship with them. Get them to laugh at him. Then get them to laugh at themselves. Electrifies their trust and their confidence begins to surge. Their interest in the classroom, in each other and in themselves, begins to amp. Boosting their ability to cope, to accept, to understand.

Coach was an accomplished esteem builder. A master identity finder.

And it didn't come from superficial encouragement. He found ways each student could feel successful. He didn't just help them discover things about history and English.

He helped them discover things about themselves. That was his only objective. That was the only framework he gave credence to.

When he stopped coaching four years before, all his circuits were connected to the classroom.

And, of course, he was obsessive.

His class was now on-line. He had a web site with a camera in the classroom so parents could check on their kids during the day. Web-cam. It was the pinnacle of accountability.

It wasn't his seniority that made him a leader among the faculty. It was the fact that he was pushing ahead, working extremely hard, relentless, pushing his convictions on everyone.

His energy seemed boundless. These last few years he recharged, and he raced to the finish line.

He had made a difference.

At times, to his surprise, he even felt good about himself.

"May your hands always by busy,
May your feet always be swift,
May you have a strong foundation
When the winds of changes shift.
May your heart always be joyful,
May your song always be sung,
And may you stay, forever young."

Why could Coach work again? He was forgetting.
The memory was dying.
Sometimes when it returned it didn't have a face. Sometimes he couldn't remember what Parker looked like. That scared him and that alone was another source of guilt.

Should I look at some photographs. Look at a video. I haven't done that since. . . .

Now sometimes, for a few hours, maybe the better part of a day he could forget.

"Forever young, forever young,
May you stay, forever young."

Joanie had removed all the pictures from the walls. It took them years before they put his things away in his room. Still, they rarely went in there.
The videos were in a box in the basement. They never spoke of him anymore. Coach never thought there would be any normalcy in his life again. There would never be recovery.
Comfort.
The mourning and despair, that would go on forever.
But there was some.
Surprisingly, more for Coach than for Joanie.
Things could never be like it was. But for the last few years Coach had endured. In many ways, more so than Joanie.

He managed to end his coaching career with a winning season. And now he also had ended his teaching career with feelings of success.

"Forever young, forever young,
May you stay, forever young."

The song ended, and the crowd erupted.
A standing ovation by the graduates.
Most were standing because the song was finally over. A short graduation speech by most standards. The administration and school board politely smiled and gave him a golf clap. The young new principal was doing the same.

Another elderly elephant was leaving the herd, departing for the bone yard, she thought, thank goodness.

There was some anxiety at the end. Some trepidation. Coach never thought there would be, but there were doubts.

I'm old, but am I too old? I love teaching. It might be the only thing that keeps me together. Keeps me hanging on.

When he left coaching four years earlier, he was worried that the last few years would slow down too much. Coaching had kept him so occupied from November to March. That time of year used to fly by.

Boy, I sometimes wondered if I would make it without coaching. Could I make it to retirement without it? Make it to the tape in one piece without coaching?

But he had made it.
Mostly by rededicating himself to living. He even regained some of his physical conditioning. Began eating more responsibly. Stopped eating sugar. Stopped drinking diet coke. Dropped a few pounds. Was jogging and biking some again.

Listening to a CD walkman. He was working in the yard. Trimming the roses. Pulling weeds.

Things took a little longer to get done, but they got done. Now, the question in his mind was, what would replace teaching? Not working was going to leave a huge void in his life. It was a scary thought.

One thing was for sure. His faith had resurrected him. Opened up his grave.

He had made it. Made it to retirement. Had a long career. Provided for a family. Maybe touched a few lives.

And it was a result of him clinging to his faith.

He knew that without the good Lord's help he wouldn't have made it. He might be heading for extinction. Maybe even extinction without significance. But he believed he was going to heaven when this was over.

Heaven. "Knockin on Heavens Door." Hey that's Dylan too. Encore anyone? Heaven. I'm ready. That might be the only way I see. . . .

But the fact remained, retirement scared him. Sometimes he even dreaded weekends. Dreaded vacations. Now he wondered if his mind would be occupied enough? No routine made him irritable and anxious.

Doesn't everyone feel this way at the end? Aren't we all institutionalized at the end?

He knew he was a working class hero. It was going to be hard to be anything else.

Michelle was turning twenty-six in a week.

She was getting married in August.

Joanie and Coach used to joke that she would follow in her mom's footsteps someday, and she had. Three years at Sierra.

Four years at Cal State and a masters degree in Speech Pathology.

Her fiancee had gotten a secondary teaching credential in science. He was a good kid. A swimmer-skier-water-polo player-hiker-camper guy. He had gotten Michelle active in the outdoors. They were a great couple. They were now living together in Sacramento. He was substitute teaching while Michelle was finishing her internship.

This summer they would both be busy interviewing for jobs. Michelle could go almost anywhere because of demand. It wouldn't be that easy for her fiancee. He did have an interview down the road at Wolf River, Coach's old nemesis. One of his old arch rivals. Jobs there would put them both in the area. Almost neighbors.

That would be great for Joanie.

Michelle and Joanie were very close. They were always close. There hadn't even been a teen separation. Very little fighting. It was more than mother and daughter. They were best friends. Coach was envious.

He never felt like a real father to Michelle.

To Michelle, he was just another of mom's boyfriends.

Another boyfriend who took mom's time away. But this boyfriend had stayed. A Tahoe wedding with Michelle as the maid of honor.

Coach had tried to get closer to Michelle. But he knew he hadn't tried hard enough. Once again, too much time spent trying to win basketball games.

It certainly wasn't easy. Marriage was all new territory to be explored, let alone being a step-dad. Adjusting to marriage was tough enough. There were some rocky roads. In the first three years he packed twice. She packed once.

Michelle and Coach were never close. He just couldn't connect with her. Most of the time he got rejected. And his attempts to win her love and admiration became awkward. Seemed too contrived.

They never hugged.

Coach even shared his concern with some of his closest friends.

Maybe she didn't feel like she measured up? Wasn't a Warrior. A hooper. An athlete. The truth? He probably didn't pay her enough attention.

She was a cheerleader and a dancer in school, and he was extremely proud of her. But she wasn't one of Coach's Amazons.

However, he was not about to give up.

Be patient.

It might take awhile, he thought, but eventually she would see his true colors.

In time. Give it more time. Maybe in her late twenties. Or thirties. She'll think of me as her father. Just be patient. Be there every day. Take care of her mother. Be loyal. Be faithful. That will account for something in the long run. The fact that I stayed. I cared. And I love her for who she is. That will eventually mean something. She will eventually recognize that.

But then Parker.

Joanie tried so hard not to blame him. But that wasn't the case with Michelle. She loved Parker very deeply. As much as a parent could. Her grief was as deep. She blamed Coach. And she hated him for it. There would be no forgiveness.

Now he would go gently.

Quietly.

Move into retirement with no fanfare. No hoopla. Most of the faculty that were hired around the same time as Coach had already done the same. And he didn't want to partake in any celebration. Especially with a bunch of teachers that he didn't know and who really didn't know him personally.

The standing ovation he received at the last faculty meeting was emotional for him. Even though most of the current faculty didn't have a clue as to who he was, they respected the fact that he had a long career. Thirty-five years at Empire.

But he still wondered. Was longevity worth all that? What about professionalism?

This last year of teaching had forced him to look back, to evaluate. Retrospection. Review.

For so many years, he was a coach. That's where most of his energy went.

Winning. Had to win.

But what about the classroom?

And after Parker.

Remember the rules! Remember the rules!

In order to survive he never looked back. He couldn't look back. That was one of his rules. Don't look back. Not by the year, or by the day.

Just go on.

Go forward.

Do the best you can.

The second rule was never look too far ahead. Never count the days. That would kill you.

Don't look back. Don't look ahead.

That way days might be slow. But the weeks would fly by. Years would fly by.

Rule number three was not too start feeling to self important. After all, it wasn't a game. Nothing to win here. Winning didn't matter. It was the relationships that really mattered in the classroom and on the court. That's all that mattered. That's what education was all about. Same as life.

Survive one day at a time.

Ironically that is what being an alcoholic taught him.

Don't try to control what can't be controlled and know the difference between the two. Not knowing what the future holds, but knowing who holds the future.

Coach was graduating.

But he knew this was not supposed to be his graduation alone. He was supposed to be sharing it.

Sharing it with Parker.

2002.
This would have been his graduation too.

Robe and mortar. Watching his dad make a fool of himself in front of all his buddies.

One last time.

One of them ending.
One of them beginning.

Forever Young.

CHAPTER SIX

APRIL 16, 1988

SATURDAY MORNING

Joanie Peterson taught Coach humility. If he had any, it was because of her.

Sometimes her lessons were brutal.

No matter how you cut it, winning was ego gratification. It's very easy for any successful coach to become full of himself. Coaches who become full of themselves eventually become full of something else too.

At awards banquets Coach used to always say that his wife was the best point guard he ever had, because she never failed to point out what he was doing wrong.

The truth was that Joanie knew the game and was very perceptive about players' attitudes and their motives. She was a constant and reliable reference able to give him a better perspective on almost everything. Coach relied on her advice on all important decisions regarding school and the Warriors.

Joanie was also persistent about demanding that Coach keep basketball in perspective. She was always reminding him of what his priorities should be.

Being a good father. Husband. Son. Brother. And teacher. Those things were far more important than winning any basketball game. Although the amount of wins, awards, achievements and recognition grew throughout the years, she remained unimpressed.

Sometimes it drove Coach crazy. But as much as he some-times hated to admit it, she was right. In the big picture, there were more important things in life. Her attitude tempered his ego and fortified his modesty.

That Saturday morning in April came one of those "prior-ity" reminders.

It was nothing but blue skies in Gold County, and Coach would have liked nothing more than to climb on his mountain bike, strap on his walkman and rock 'n roll down some Sierra trail.

Before getting married to Joanie, before Michelle and Parker, he might have been getting some exercise out on the golf course or on the tennis court. But there just wasn't time for those forms of recreational exercise anymore.

Now if Coach could squeeze an hour out of a day, he spent it grinding away out in the woods by himself. No tee-time or court reservation needed. Weather permitting and a break in his family's demands . . . Coach loved to ride his bike.

However, on this Saturday morning, the Peterson's had loaded up the mini van and headed for the Arden Fair Mall in Sacramento.

It was a family excursion to shop for spring and summer clothes for Michelle and Parker. Coach's primary job was al-ways to watch Parker while Joanie and Michelle did most of the shopping. That suited him just fine. Coach hated shopping.

The drive from the foothills of the Gold County was roughly sixty miles.

With the windy roads leaving Empire and the Sacramento city traffic, it usually took an hour and a half to reach the downtown mall.

Coach had just spent what seemed like the last four months driving the school van to games in the valley. Although Empire was a small town in itself, the high school was large. Students from all the surrounding little gold rush towns and white flight gated communities were bused, driven, or drove themselves to Empire High to attend classes. Because the area had grown so much since Coach began teaching there twenty-one years ago, the school had well over twenty-five hundred students. The enrollment was too large to compete against other smaller Northern California towns, so they were forced to play in the Capital League in Sacramento.

That meant logging a considerable amount of miles. Parents had to volunteer to drive players. Coach would drive a van, taking some players, the equipment, and his assistant, Willie Dutroy. It was more convenient, less time consuming and cheaper than commandeering a school bus.

Coach, like he always was at this time of the year, was exhausted.

He didn't have that "got his butt kicked out of the playoffs" post season depression this year, but he was tired.

He always hated to see the season end.

He loved coaching. Loved the game.

And when it was time to get off the high wire he came down hard, both physically and mentally. It took a while to recover.

This year there hadn't been much of a chance to rest at the end of the season. They had just won the State Championship.

There were victory parades, banquets, photos, and speaking engagements. He was running on empty. But the euphoria of having won State the month before hadn't yet subsided. And he doubted it ever would.

The one concession Joanie had made was that she offered to drive. Coach was navigating. Parker was strapped in the second seat. Michelle and her friend Becky were in the back.

To Coach's lament, they were leaving a cushy blue sky in the foothills to spend a self-denying demanding day at the mall in the city.

Days like this always reminded Coach how lucky he was to live in such a beautiful place.

It was an extraordinary coincidence that had landed him in the Sierra foothills.

The Gold County was a vibrantly remote area. It remained unknown to most Californians, let alone a cheesehead from Wisconsin like himself. He had been familiar with the history of the gold rush in California, but not so much with its geography. So after graduating from the University of Wisconsin, he loaded up his ol' '55 and headed west to visit his sister.

Off he went. With no real expectations, and no real game plan.

His sister, who had just gotten married, moved up from San Francisco where she had been working as a nurse. Her new husband, whom she had recently met in the Bay Area, sold real estate, and he saw an opportunity to cash in on the population explosion that was taking place in the Sierras. The white flight to the Northern California foothills was booming. People were moving up in droves from Southern California, the Bay Area and Sacramento

The rarely used 6'2" shooting guard for the University of Wisconsin Badgers had only been offered two interviews for teaching and coaching positions in Wisconsin. And from those two interviews he didn't get a job offer. So he figured if he was going to have to try and make a living substitute teaching, instead of returning to his home town of Twin Rivers, Wisconsin, he would accept an offer from his older sister and bunk in the granny house out behind their newly purchased property in Empire. Do something a little more exciting, something a little more adventurous.

In early September, 1966, his old Chevy was on the road heading west. California dreaming.

He felt he could use a change of scenery anyway.

And what he found there twenty-two years ago was a Mecca for outdoor fun: wonderfully fresh mountain rivers, lakes, hiking trails and golf courses. It was close to Lake Tahoe for skiing and gambling. It also had a growing high school that needed substitute teachers almost daily. Soon he rented a cabin and began enjoying himself. At the end of one year he was hired full time as an English teacher and the junior varsity boys basketball coach.

In the ensuing years, meanwhile, his sister Christina, moved down to San Diego, got divorced, remarried, and then moved back to Green Bay, Wisconsin.

Coach Peterson had arrived with very few possessions, just a suitcase and an old Chevrolet. But a problem he had hoped to leave behind him had hitched a ride.

Coach Peterson had a drinking problem.
In fact, he was an alcoholic.

Alcoholism is progressive with age, and Coach's drinking grew worse.
He first suspected he might have a problem way back in his first year of college.
He experienced blackouts.
After nights drinking with the team at the Delta Frat House or at the bars down on State Street, the next morning he would realize there were parts missing. Sometimes hours were missing.

This began to scare him.
It was his scary little secret kept from his friends and teammates. His friends were joking about things he did that he couldn't remember. Funny stories. Hah hah. They all laughed, loved them. But not Coach. He couldn't believe he actually did the things they were saying. He tried not to show it. He'd laugh along. But he was secretly filled with guilt, shame, and embarrassment. He agonized over it. He knew there was something wrong.
Something was definitely wrong!

Once he even snuck down to the school infirmary to talk to a counselor. The counselor told him he was probably drinking to excess because of stress: exam anxiety and the weight of having to sit on the bench for a losing team.

Coach often thought about how things could have been different if that counselor had diagnosed what any counselor worth his salt should have known especially, if he had looked into Coach's family history. He never even asked! Coach's family tree was full of drunks. Relatives who had died young from the affects of alcohol. Some died very violently under the influence.

He tried to control his drinking on his own. But his attempts, of course, were fruitless and ineffective.

The blackouts continued. The embarrassing incidents increased.

After two years as the boys' junior varsity coach, he moved to the varsity.

The former Head Coach took the job as the principal. Coach had won at the junior varsity level; now it was his chance to show he could do it at the varsity level.

He was young, talented, and lucky.

In his first year as the Varsity Coach, he inherited a very athletic group, and they played for the section title, losing in a very close game for the Championship. The kids loved him. And the parents got used to his intensity. The program began to grow.

So did his drinking.

In April after his third season, he was arrested for drunk driving.

The arrest was listed in the police blotter in the local paper. It was in small print but was a huge embarrassment. Kurtis Posny, the new principal, and ex-Head Coach, gave him a stern warning.

Most of his colleagues supported him. Most of them all agreed, "It could happen to anyone."

"Who hasn't had a few too many and driven home?"

"Didn't it only take just a coupla beers to be legally drunk anyway?"

Three years later, almost to the day, it happened again. DUI.

This time because of his now growing notoriety in the community, he got headlines. Second page news. Large print.

Now it was obvious. He was a lush and a growing liability to the school's standing in the community. Fellow faculty members were calling for his head. The principal was taken out of the loop. It went to the top. The District Superintendent, Michael Elmhurst, told coach to get a lawyer.

The lawyer, a hot shot from Sacramento, saved his credential with the state teachers' licensing board and the school board couldn't fire him.

Besides the fine, he was sentenced to ten days in jail, put on probation, had his driving license suspended for a year and required to attend counseling.

Coach had hit the bottom.

He considered many options.

Suicide was one of them.

He was alone. Had no one to turn to. No family. He was too ashamed to tell his parents. In the state of California if he was arrested a third time for drunk driving he would be charged with a felony, an automatic loss of his teaching credential for life, and a minimum of 180 days in jail.

The arresting officer almost let him go. Coach begged him.

"You know who I am. This is going to ruin me. You've got to give me a break."

The officer decided he was way too intoxicated and took him to jail.

It didn't ruin his life.

It saved it.

Coach had a choice. Continue with the ancient family tradition or surrender.

He surrendered.

The booze was too powerful. He realized it could not be defeated. He always believed that you learn more from loosing than from winning. Now the lesson that he learned would change his life forever.

From the night he was arrested a second time, and for the remainder of his life, he never drank alcohol again. Not one single drop.

Even though his life would change tragically on that April day in 1988, one month after winning the State Championship, he would remain sober forever.

Coach put in one more season as the boy's varsity coach and then resigned citing personal reasons. The personal reasons, of course, were to try and get sober.

The road to recovery was a rough one. Humbling to say the least, from the front page of the sports section where he was a respected and accomplished coach to picking up trash on weekends in the park as part of his community service sentence. He cleaned up garbage Saturday and Sunday in one of the local parks in lieu of his ten days in jail.

He attended mandatory AA meetings.

He walked or rode the bus. During his last season as the boy's varsity coach, he waited until everyone left the gym and the locker room and then walked the two miles home, sometimes in the rain and snow. Many times not arriving home until after midnight.

One day at a time. He began to make his stand.

New rules! Don't look ahead. Don't look back. Those are the rules! The rules!

Deep down inside he knew that alcohol had always prevented him from becoming the person he wanted to be. Now he didn't have a choice. He had come to California to escape, only to discover that where you are doesn't make a bit of difference, it's what you are that matters. He was an alcoholic and now he was forced to make a choice.

His drinking friends soon faded away, and some days were excruciatingly lonely. Coach kept up his appearances with his family back in Wisconsin. He never once shared what his new life's focus was.

Get sober.

Stay sober.

He never envisioned how quickly things would get better. There were still the funny looks from people in the community. There were still the rumors of past drug use and womanizing.

Some were true, most were not.

Almost instantly he became more organized, better prepared, and more effective in the classroom. His confidence gradually began to return.

And then he met Joanie.

One of his former players kept teasing him about his divorced older sister.

He had met her briefly after that final season ending team banquet.

Coach had been impressed.

She was gorgeous. Loved sports. Intelligent. A speech pathologist at two county middle schools.

He wanted to ask her out but he had cold feet.

Too many skeletons in the closet.

Besides, he hadn't been on a date since high school. He wasn't even sure how to act on one. Hadn't been with a woman sober since high school.

Out of the blue, she called him up and asked if he would like
to go out. On a date! But he declined.
She called again. He accepted.
Two years later in the summer of 1978, he married her.
Coach not only became a husband but a father too. Joanie
had a wonderful little two-year-old girl from a previous marriage.
Later that fall he was asked to end his two year hiatus and
return to coaching. This time as the girls' junior varsity Coach.
Humbling.
But it was a chance to get back in the gym, back on the court.
Besides they needed someone, and the principal asked him to
do it as a favor. Coach felt he owed him. So he agreed. Two years
later he became the girls' varsity coach and would remain so for
the next eighteen years.

The three of them together, Joanie, Michelle, and Coach,
could have lived happily ever after, and he would have been
eternally grateful.

But in 1985 along came Parker.

For Coach it was like he had never known true happiness.
Joy.
Everything about it, the pregnancy, the birth, the baby.
For Coach it was like a gift from Heaven, a gift from God.

*A few years ago I was going to do myself in. Leave for the Texas oil
fields. How could someone who only a few years earlier was going to
commit seppuku be so blessed?*

Parker changed Coach.
Things that were so very important before no longer had
the significance they once had.
Like winning.

Because of Parker, teaching became more important. He cared more about the kids and less about winning, even though his success as a girls' coach began to grow.

He truly cared. He was much more tolerant. Patient.

Now kids and students could do no wrong. They were someone else's babies.

His students and players recognized it too. They always respected him, were thankful and appreciative for the wins, for his time, their popularity in school and the community, but now it was more.

They knew he genuinely cared about them. As people. As individuals.

Coach adored Parker. He took him everywhere.

His life seemed complete.

CHAPTER SEVEN

APRIL 16, 1988

SATURDAY AFTERNOON

There would not be another day in Coach's life that he wouldn't be forced to remember the events of this particular afternoon.

He was given the cruelest and possibly the most inhumane punishment given any man.

It wasn't confinement.

There were no bars.

It was just a memory.

But there was no escape.

No parole.

And the sentence was life.

No matter where Coach went, no matter where he was, the awful memory would find him. Sometimes it would come in broad daylight. It would suffocate him and leave him gasping for breath.

Was it a heart attack? A heart attack wouldn't be so bad. Dying wouldn't be so bad. A relief. Wouldn't it be a relief? I've lived long enough anyway. I'm tired of living. Enough already.

At night it would awaken and remind him that he lived in a world where victims received the punishment and criminals went free.

Sometimes it would trick him into thinking it was growing weary of the haunt. Maybe he had enough. But then something would happen to remind him. The flood gates would open. And the memory would pour in and begin to drown him again.

The memory just kept coming and coming and coming. Bringing the same question. Day after day, week after week, month after month, year after year: What if. . . . What if. . . . What if. . . ?

Sometime it felt like a bad dream. His whole life had turned into a bad dream. A long and terrible nightmare where he couldn't wake up. His past, a terrible memory; his future, more torture.

Joanie pulled the van into the Arden Mall parking lot and swung around back to the parking garage.

She liked to call it her "secret spot." Sure enough there was an empty space on the lower level near one of the back entrances.

Last minute plans were formulated. They would all grab a bite to eat at the mall food court, and then Joanie, Michelle, and Becky would go shopping for clothes for Michelle. After Michelle was done, it would be Parker's turn. While the three of them were busy, Coach and Parker would bum around the mall. Coach would take Parker into the Disney Store, Warner Bros., and the FAO Swartz Toy Store. Each hour on the hour they would rendezvous on the benches outside Macy's.

The five of them ate quickly; the two girls were too excited to sit around in the food court for very long.

"Bye-bye Parker. Give Mom a kiss and a hug," Joanie said. The girls had finished eating and were getting ready to shove off. "Now keep an eye on Parker. Don't you let him out of your sight, Pete. Parker, we'll see you in a little bit. Be a good boy."

Joanie gave them both a hug and hurried after the girls who had already started walking down the mall.

Coach and Parker took the escalator down to the bottom floor from the food court. Parker was always fascinated by the escalators, and you couldn't go by one in the mall without going up or down it, as the case might be. Coach figured he would be doing a lot of escalator riding before the afternoon was over.

The first store they came to was the toy store. Coach thought there was a pretty good chance they might be spending the first hour in this one alone. Parker loved the store. The talking tree, robotic dinosaur, and the roaring lion. The store was a playground for Parker. He laughed and played running from one thing to the next. His excitement always got the attention of other shoppers as well as the kids who worked there. They would bring him things to look at and play with. Coach was very proud of how polite, how appreciative he was about all the attention he got.

Fifty minutes flew by.

It was time to head for Macy's and their first rendezvous with the girls. With Parker hanging onto Coach's hand, they stopped to look at the new athletic shoe display in the doorway of Footlocker. Fascination with athletic footwear. It was a jock trait.

Coach never remembered letting go of Parker's hand to pick up the shoe.

He examined it, and put it back on the stand. Without looking, he reached down for Parker's hand.

Nothing happened.

Coach looked down. Parker wasn't there.

He quickly glanced in both directions. Looked in the store, then down the mall.

Panic, now don't panic. This has happened before. You've lost sight of him before. Remember that time in the front yard when he was two. You began to panic, and he had just walked around the side of the garage. You started yelling and Joanie came out and scolded you for losing sight of him. No, don't panic. He's right here.

But Coach couldn't see him.

"Parker," Coach said out loud.

"Parker," a little louder this time.

Wait, he must have spotted Joanie or Michelle walking by. He's right outside here. Don't yell.

He wasn't outside.

"Parker, where are you? Excuse me, did you see where my boy went, a little guy?" Coach asked a pimply faced kid in a referee shirt. He just looked at Coach without saying a word. He was busy showing some guy the new Air Jordan's.

Go ahead. Ignore me. What kind of father loses his son anyway?

Coach ran back out of the store.

"Parker!" Now he was yelling. Now he didn't care that people might begin to stare.

"Parker!" another even louder. Didn't care if his wife heard. Or even if she saw him from around the corner where she might be standing, with Parker, and the girls, ready to scold him again.

"Parker! Parker!" He was becoming terrified. He was running to the doorways of the stores next to Footlocker. First one then the other, yelling.

*This isn't happening. Come on. This can't be happening! Please,
Parker. Daddy doesn't care how foolish he might look. Just come out
Parker. Daddy isn't mad.*

Now two security guards were walking rapidly toward
him. One was talking into his walkie talkie. A small crowd was
beginning to form, staring at him.

"Calm down, sir," said one of the security guards.

"Calm down?" The question that came from Coach's mouth
could hardly be heard, his mouth was too dry. He was trying
hard now to fight the hysteria that was beginning to swallow
him.

Parker has to be right here! He has to be! He was just here!

"He was right here a minute ago," Coach said looking at the
two guards.

"Calm down, sir," one of the guards repeated.

"Parker!" at the top of his lungs. The security guard was
reaching for him. Reaching out for his arm.

"Parker!" Coach continued to yell even louder.

Half way down the mall Joanie was coming out of a clothing
store. She thought she heard someone yelling Parker's name.
She stopped to listen.

Then she heard it loud and clear.

"No," was all she said before she began to run in the
direction from where it came.

"Parker!" Coach was crying. "Why aren't you helping me?
Let go of me! He was just here! He was just here!" Coach was
losing it now. Panic attack. He could hardly breathe. When
Joanie got to Coach, the security guards were holding onto him,
holding him up, trying to get some information, a description.

"He was just here!" Coach kept repeating. "He was just here!"

But he wasn't

Parker was gone.

CHAPTER EIGHT

FEBRUARY 24, 2004

TUESDAY MORNING

Coach told Joanie he found Parker on the cover of *Sports Illustrated*.

He showed her the cover photo of Lester Travis. Told her about his suspicions. He tried to share the article but he never got that far.

She fell apart.
She begged him to get help.

She couldn't believe her life was still continuing to spiral downward. After sixteen years! Sixteen years since Parker disappeared. The therapist told her it would never get better. But it would change. But change for the worse?

"Did the article say he was adopted, Pete? Do you think Edward Travis, famous movie producer, stole our son? What are you going to do, Pete? Call him up and ask for him back? They are going to lock you up!"

Coach sat alone in his study. No TV. No computer. Joanie had left for work late.

She was still crying when she walked out the door.

Am I crazy? I couldn't handle the alcohol. It took a long time to accept that. But I finally gave up. Is this the same thing? Am I crazy?

I can't handle this. I can't handle this. My wife. She's always right. Another panic attack. Second one in two days. She's right. I'm going to kill myself. Another disease. This one maybe even worse. Why hasn't this killed me yet?

He picked up the phone and called the doctor's office. He made an appointment.

Maybe all I need is some medication. Maybe a referral. Talk to a specialist. A shrink. They have drugs for loonies like me.

He went upstairs, showered and shaved. After he rinsed his face he stared for a long time at himself in the mirror. An old man stared back. A stranger stared back.

Who is this guy? Who is this old man? None of my students used to come within ten years of guessing my age. I can't remember ever looking this old. My belly shakes when I brush my teeth. I'm losing the battle. Haven't exercised in three months. I've rarely missed a day the last forty years. Mind and body. That's what's wrong. I need to bike. Jog. That would kick out the jam. Wake me up. I'll do that as soon as I get back from seeing the doctor. They will make me get on the scale. Weigh me. That will be incentive enough. Have to regain some balance. Balance.

He went to the bedroom and began to get dressed. Opened the drawer next the bed, and took out his prayer book. He knelt beside the bed, and began to read some of his favorite prayers.

Don't let me lose Joanie. She is all I've got left. Please don't take her away from me.

He got up and started to put on his shoes.

Stay active. That's the key. Exercise. Take Joanie to the movies. Clean the house. Cook dinner. Take her out to dinner. Tonight. Time to cut back those roses. Need to get started. Plan a trip. Maybe Mexico?

Cabo? Where I asked her to marry me? Maybe go in August on our anniversary? Surprise her with the tickets. Dad enjoyed over twenty years of retirement. The key is to stay active. Stay active.

Some research wouldn't hurt though.
A little investigation. See what the net could come up with.

Joanie didn't have to know.

How would she know?

CHAPTER NINE

MARCH 14, 2004

SUNDAY MORNING

What started out as a whim grew to be another one of Coach's obsessions.

At first it was just something to do. It was interesting just to see what he could come up with. Now it had become more than that. No matter how many dead end roads he went down, no matter how frustrated he became, he spent all his time on it.

If he wasn't working the internet, he was thinking about other avenues to pursue. He went to bed with it. And he woke up with it.

He found nothing.

No evidence.

But the more he worked at it, for some reason he became more and more convinced that Lester Travis, a collegiate basketball star and son of a famous movie producer, was Parker.

He ignored the hard core evidence. He had Parker's fingerprints. He had Lester's fingerprints. They were not a match.

The fact that he could find this all out over the internet amazed him. Fascinated him.

Practically everything he went after, he found.

He had hospital records. Copies of birth certificates. Financial records, tax returns, school records, phone bills, credit card expenditures. His file on the Travis family grew daily.

Seems nothing about a person is safe anymore. Privacy? No such animal. Endangered species. Extinct.

He accessed programs run by other internet snoops. He was exchanging e-mail information with them. They offered their services, for a fee, of course. They were thieves. Criminals. Some of them were actually in prison. They told Coach where to go and how to get there. Most were low-life's. They were despicable characters, who wished him well in his "rip-off" attempt.

At times he felt very dirty.

But it didn't stop him from looking.

He had no intention of ripping anyone off, but if Edward Travis had committed a crime, if somehow Lester was Parker, then he had to continue his investigation until he was satisfied.

Joanie knew nothing. She always thought he was a little wacky anyway, but this was way out there. Even Coach recognized it as being pretty absurd.

But he couldn't stop.

He even went as far as to obtain a credit card that he was hiding from Joanie. Running down to the mailbox everyday so she wouldn't find the statement in the mail. He needed it to pay his way into certain places on the net. And even though he knew it was risky to give out a credit card number on the net, it was necessary. It would only be temporary, he thought. Then he would cancel and destroy it. He thought of himself as an undercover hacker. And his dossier on Edward Travis began to bulge.

Edward Travis graduated from a high school in Indiana.

He graduated at the top of his class, valedictorian, and received numerous scholarships. He decided to go to Western Pacific and major in film production. It wasn't long before his talent and creativity began to impress both his professors and classmates. It didn't surprise anyone that with his aptitude and artistic vision, combined with his boundless energy, that he would produce films even before graduating. During his senior year, some of his fellow classmates and himself, under his direction of course, pooled their resources and began to make low budget films. Plenty of sex and violence. It wasn't long before they were all making money, living in rented beach houses and driving sports cars.

After graduation he began to produce films on his own. He made billions. Soon after his first solo production he met an aspiring young actress, Rebecca Cannon. They met one night at a Hollywood party. After two months of a wild romantic escapade they were married in Las Vegas.

They only had one child. Lester.

Edward Travis had become a very wealthy and powerful man, not just because of his success in the film industry. Through his many large political contributions, he was very well connected. Maybe all the way to the top, not just in California, but in Washington D.C. as well.

His tax returns were very complicated. There were a lot of people on his payroll.

Travis' wife Rebecca was extremely attractive. Movie star looks and a movie star body.

She was from Southern California from a modest family that owned an asphalt paving business. When they met she was attending nursing school and at the same time auditioning for bit movie roles. She was ten years younger than Travis. Only nineteen when they met. She knew who Edward Travis was from some of the movie sets he visited.

"What a catch he would be," she thought. A young rich movie producer.

All it took was a wild party in the hills. Mission accomplished.

She loved the money.

While Travis was out making it, she was busy spending it. She spent most of her time globe-trotting and hob knobbing with the rich and famous. There were many pictures of her in movie magazines attending parties, awards ceremonies and premieres. She had become a fixture at some of the all night dance clubs around town. She wrecked expensive automobiles and there was some hot gossip about her infidelity. Rumors abounded about her many trysts and affairs with some of Edward Travis' leading men.

Edward, on the other hand, had grown to be much less pretentious. Quiet. Elusive. All business. No nonsense.

A workaholic. He dressed rather modestly and had much less extravagant tastes. It seemed he no longer liked the spotlight as much as his wife did. Many times he didn't even bother to attend the premieres of his own movies. He was too busy moving on to his next project.

His business deals and various investments were diverse and complex.

He didn't limit himself to just making movies anymore. He owned whole companies and parts of others. He was a hands on manager. Crafty, and shrewd. Ruthless. It appeared to Coach that he didn't just enjoy the satisfaction that went with making movies, he was obsessed with the business of making money.

If Edward Travis had committed a crime, Coach believed, he had the money and the power to cover it up.

Records could easily be fabricated. There was tons of information on the internet, but there was just as much misinformation. Anything could be thrown up there. I just need a clue. Something that doesn't jive. Just a hint of a some cover up. A grassy knoll with a second shooter. I need something. Then I can take to my feet. Travel if necessary. Get hard copy. Get primary sources.

When Coach returned from church, he found the house empty.

Joanie left a note saying she had gone walking with some friends.

Today the NCAA brackets were to be announced. Coach waited in his study watching the end of the last college conference championship. Afterward the network would televise the announcement of the tournament brackets. Western Pacific was still in a position to receive a number one seed. If that were the case they would probably be chosen to head up the Western Region. The first round was going to be played at the Oakland Coliseum.

The phone in his study rang.

Since it was Sunday, Coach expected it to be either his mother or one of his sisters. It was usually on Sunday when they took time to check up on each other.

However, it was a man's voice that spoke. "Mr. Peterson?" Coach's first thought was that it was a salesman. A phone solicitor.

On a Sunday! They're calling on Sundays now!

"Yes." Coach's response was curt.

"Mr. Peterson, I work for a legal securities service. We've discovered that you are participating in a great deal of illegal activity."

Coach was quickly shook up by the sudden accusation. He could feel his heart beat begin to increase. A blood flow rushed to his head. But at the same time he tried to remain defensive.

"Yeah, what illegal activity is that?" Coach asked.

"You are accessing information that is illegal. Illegal and private," the man said.

"Can you be a little more specific? What information is that?" Coach asked again.

There was a long hesitation before a response came.

"Look Peterson, you're stalking. You know exactly what the hell I'm talking about. You're stalking one of my clients. And if it doesn't subsist we're going to take legal action. Or worse."

His tone had abruptly changed It no longer sounded in the least bit professional. Far from being diplomatic.

Coach was being threatened.

The man continued, "There are laws against stalking you know, and if it continues then you, and your little wife..."

Suddenly another man came on the line. Interrupted.

"Mr. Peterson. Hello. Mr. Peterson. Look Mr. Peterson, my associate sometimes tends to get a little too excited. What he is trying to say is simply this." His voice was much calmer, cold, and calculated. "Our clients wish to maintain their privacy at all costs. They pay my agency a lot of money to guard their privacy and preserve their security. If that privacy is breached then it is our job to use whatever means to resecure it. Believe me Mr. Peterson, we have a lot more tools and resources than you want to imagine. We believe you have taken a particular interest in one of our clients, and it is our desire that you subsist. Or, like my associate indicated, serious action will be taken. Action, that quite frankly, could be very damaging to you and your family. We are prepared to take a very swift and a very firm stand on this matter."

There was a slight hesitation, and then he added. "Do you understand?"

"Yes." Coach was now scared. Very scared.

"Good, then we can all assume there will be no need to talk again. Have a nice day," he added, and hung up.

Coach slowly put the phone back on the hook. He was shaking.

Now what have I done? What have I become? Joanie was right. This is lunacy. I need help. I need a drink. A cigarette. I've put my family in jeopardy all because of some absurd notion, one that I'm not sure I even believe. This isn't some game. The man is right. What I'm doing might be legal, but it isn't moral. Or normal. How did they know? Was I ratted out by another snoop? Are there ways of knowing who is getting what over the internet? I'm stalking a family. What kind of pathetic looser would do something like this? I have a secret file on my computer. I'm keeping it a secret from my wife. Putting her in danger. Putting Michelle in danger. What exactly am I doing?

He was watching them.

And now they were watching him.

The NCAA Tournament Brackets were being announced on the TV.

The Western Pacific Pirates were the number one seed in the West.

They would play the number sixteen seed, the University of Texas-El Paso, in the first round.

On Thursday.

At the Oakland Coliseum.

CHAPTER TEN

MARCH 15, 2004

MONDAY EVENING

Sara Rick, one of Coach's ex-players, was a blood relative of Michelle's.

Sara's mother was Joanie's ex-sister-in-law. Joanie had been married to Sara's uncle, which made Michelle and Sara cousins. Things like that happen in small towns.

Sara was a great player.

And even a better student. Graduated second in her class. 4.0. A Valedictorian.

She went to the University of California-Davis as an undergraduate, and then to Georgetown Law School where she also graduated at the top of her class. She immediately got a job as a special prosecutor for the federal government.

She was one of Coach's all time favorite players.

A brilliant kid who cussed like a sailor. A tough competitor who constantly made big plays in big games. What she lacked in ability she made up for with spirit, hard work and desire.

She loved the game. She was a student of the game. She wasn't born with a silver spoon in her mouth either. Mom was divorced and had to work full-time as a travel agent. Sara had to work too. She had jobs all through high school. She knew what a dollar was worth. Wasn't spoiled. Very appreciative for her age.

She also had a wonderful sense of humor which made her a joy to be around. Although it had been years since she played, years since she moved away, when she came to town to visit her mother and brother she always went out of her way to stop by and visit.

Sara loved sports. Especially basketball.

She was a hoop junkie just like Coach.

He loaned her tons of his basketball books and videos. As an undergraduate at UC-Davis she even went to clinics with Coach and his staff so she could hear some of the collegiate legends speak. The masters. Bobby Knight, Rick Pitino, Nolan Richardson, Dick Bennett, Rick Majerus, and Pat Summit, were all favorites of hers.

Between speakers she would hang around the casino sports bar in South Lake Tahoe, or where ever the clinic was being held, smoke cigars and talk hoop with all the other coaches.

Coach really got a kick out of her interest and her respect for the game.

But most of all he loved the fact that she still took time out to visit his family. Although she had become a big time attorney and traveled all over the world, she hadn't changed much. She never forgot Michelle's birthday. She never forgot Michelle at Christmas.

Coach also knew that Joanie loved her as much as he did. He knew that she enjoyed hearing from her, and seeing her just as much as he did.

On Monday night she surprised Coach with a phone call.

"Coach, I'm coming to California to get some depositions. I'll be working in San Francisco Tuesday and Wednesday. Then I'm going to drive up to see Mom."

"You're a Globe-trotter, Sara," said Coach.

"Coach I've got tickets to the NCAA regionals. You want to go?" asked Sara.

"Are you kidding? Of course I want to go," Coach answered.

"I can drive, Coach. I'm coming back up your way after the game so I can spend the weekend in Reno with my brother. I'm going to fly back to DC from Reno on Monday. So it's drive up to have dinner with Mom on Wednesday night. Back down to Oakland Thursday for the game, and then back up the hill Thursday night. And sometime Friday I leave for Reno."

"What? Is this perfect or what? I don't even have to drive? Western Pacific-UTEP, Indiana-New Mexico."

"I know. Some great hoop Coach. One problem. I only have two tickets. Will Joanie be bummed?"

"She'll be fine. She'll be glad to see me get off my butt. Besides, she has to work. She'll be OK!" Coach said excitedly.

"You're sure, Coach?" Sara asked cautiously.

"She'll be fine. Call Wednesday night to say hi."

"OK. I can do that. I'll plan on that."

"Sara, this is great. Thanks a lot. I guess I'll see you on Thursday then."

"See you on Thursday, Coach. Give Auntie Joanie all my love. And Michelle and her new hubby, if you talk to them."

"Will do. Now don't lose those tickets!" said Coach.

"Don't worry I won't. See you Thursday around noon." Sara was laughing.

"Thursday at noon. I'll be ready. Thanks again, Sara."

"No problemo. Bye, Coach."

"Bye, Sara."

Tickets to the regionals. Wow! I have to try and relax. Enjoy myself. Try not to think about Lester Travis. Or the phone call. The whole thing is crazy anyway. Lester. Parker. Crazy. I've got to put an end to this obsession. Like the mall trips. Has to end! Put an end to it. No drinking. No smoking. No internet. Cold turkey. No addictions.

Coach Peterson felt much better about things.

Tomorrow. No computer. Maybe go for a bike ride. Rent a movie. Tonight. Ice cream. Sports Center. Fill out an NCAA tourney bracket.

Have to study up if I'm going to be talking hoop with Sara.

It will be great.

Things will be OK.

Things will be OK.

CHAPTER ELEVEN

MARCH 18, 2004

THURSDAY NIGHT

OAKLAND COLISEUM

Lester Travis was a player. Definitely a player.

Dominating.

Both offensively and defensively he was the driver of this juggernaut of future NBA players that made up the Western Pacific squad. You could tell immediately he was their captain, and there would be no letdown under his leadership. There would be no stumble in the first round.

They blew UTEP away.

Lester Travis played with tremendous intensity and focus. Even when they were ahead by twenty, he was still diving on the floor for loose balls.

He wasn't just a scorer either. He played defense. He consistently stayed down low in his stance. You rarely saw players bother to bend their knees on defense anymore, but Lester could drop his knuckles on the floor. He was right under the chin of the player he was guarding. He never used defense as an opportunity to rest. He played vigilant ballside and weakside defense. Always ready to help. He was tenacious. Stubborn. Played extremely hard on both ends of the floor.

On the offensive end he possessed great vision. His teammates worked hard to get open because they knew he would find them. He loved the pass. Sharp. No looks. He was a distributor. Instinctive. Intuitive.

He could score in bunches. Had a great shooter's touch. He could catch and nail threes. Could score off the dribble. His first step was lightning, and he used his body and shoulders to penetrate, dish, or finish with a dunk. He was Stockton, Kidd, Magic, Iverson, and Payton. Great college and NBA guards, all rolled into one.

And he was only a sophomore!

And when it was time to come out of the game and let the role players finish up, you could tell he was a little reluctant. He loved being in there in too much. But once out, he stood and cheered their efforts, even waving a towel around when his teammates made a play.

Sara and Coach agreed. It was probably his last year in college. He definitely possessed the pro game already.

How could this kid be Parker? He's extraordinary. He had to be someone's kid. But mine? You are out there, Peterson! Way out there!

Sara and Coach had great seats. They were in the corner on one end of the court, but only seven rows from the floor. They could see the faces of the players. They could hear the communication between them.

Late in the second half Western Pacific had an inbound play on its offensive end of the floor. Right in front of where they were both sitting.

Lester Travis was the player who was going to inbound the ball. Just for an instant Travis turned his head to receive the ball from the referee. From where Coach was sitting he could see his face very plainly.

A chill ran up his spine.

He could feel the hair on the back of his neck stand up.

He didn't just look like the kid in his dream! He *was* the kid in his dream!

Despite all this ability, he was still only nineteen years old, and he had the features of a nineteen year old.
So young.
The dark innocent eyes.
The hair.
The complexion.
His build. The bony shoulders, and narrow back.

He looks so young.
It's my little boy! Oh my God! It's my little boy! Parker. It's Parker! It can't be! Coincidence right? Coincidence!

Sara was saying something to Coach, but he couldn't hear her. He couldn't even hear the crowd. His ears were ringing so loudly it drowned out everything. Buzzing. Buzzing. He shrunk into almost a fetal position with his hands clasped tightly in his lap, knees pinched together, mouth draped wide open. Staring. Staring in disbelief.

Joanie's right. I've lost it. Is this my imagination? An aberration. What is this? Is this what it's like to go crazy? I have another disease. What am I? Chemicals. Chemically unbalanced? It's the same kid. It's him. In my dream. I have to be imagining this.
Oh God!
Oh God!
Help me.
Please. Help me.

For an instant he was as terrified as he was that day in the mall.
Panic. Terror. Hysteria. Taking over.
It took everything he could to maintain control. He wanted to get up, get up and run.

Just run. Run! Run home. Run!

And keep on running until you get home. Home to where Joanie is.

Home. Go home. Leave! Now!

But he hung on.
He squeezed his hands together and he hung on.
Gradually his hearing began to return.
He started to breath again
Then suddenly he began to laugh. To chuckle.
He looked over at Sara and she was looking back at him. She was laughing at him. At first Coach wondered how long she had been doing that. He was unable to hear earlier. Now he could hear her loud and clear.

"What the heck are you laughing at, Coach?" she asked.

"Nothing. Nothing. These guys are good," Coach managed to get out.

"Yeah, they're good. They might win it all," she said looking at him very curiously.

Even though the Western Pacific game was a blow out, it was entertaining. Entertaining because of Lester Travis' ability.

Indiana won at the buzzer giving their new young coach his first tourney victory and the Hoosier faithful their first tourney win in six years. Western Pacific and Indiana would now play each other on Saturday night to see who would get to go to Phoenix and take their shot at advancing to the Final Four in San Antonio.

Sara and Coach headed east on I-80 out of Oakland for the two and a half to three hour drive that would take them back up to Empire.

They listened to sports talk radio and critiqued the games they had just seen.

Their conversation turned to basketball in general. They talked about the changes in the game, the changes in coaching philosophy, and the changes in young players' attitudes.

Coach talked about the many variations, the modifications and the trends he had experienced in his tenure as a basketball coach.

How he himself had to be flexible and constantly changing to allow himself to grow with the game.

He felt that players today needed so much more freedom. Even as a high school coach, he had begun to offer that.

Players had become so much more selfish. Egotistical and self-serving. TV had a lot to do with that. The media in general. Athletes were models. Politicians. Advertising champions. Corporate trophies. They were web-sited and billboarded, their images pasted on food and fashion. Style was much more important than substance. Exposure more important than team experience. Image everything. Loyalty nothing. Today's athlete demanded respect but gave none. And today's societies the world over worshipped them.

Getting them to play together became more and more difficult throughout the years. Kids today played more for themselves, the media, agents, and their parents than they did for coaches. For high school players the cost of a college education was forcing parents to put more pressure on their son or daughter. The lessons about life that athletic competition had to offer had so many more obstacles today. Teaching was tougher than ever. Just getting them to listen was a challenge. If they didn't like what they heard or saw, they changed channels.

Many times the message they were getting from their parents was just the opposite of what a coach believed he had to teach.

Coach talked about where Sara herself had fit into that transition. The transformation of basketball and society that he experienced.

They reminisced about her senior season.

They barely made the playoffs but managed to make it to the Section Championship game before getting beat. It was Coach's period of resurgence, renewal, his rededication, and some of his best coaching ever.

They received an at-large birth to the State Tournament. Playing on the road in the first round they pulled off a miraculous upset over Bishop O'Dowd of Oakland.

Winning in overtime.

Sara hit a three pointer at the buzzer of regulation to put the game into overtime. From there they made a couple of key free throws in the final ten seconds of OT to ice it. Sara had a great all around game that night and so did Coach. The following weekend at the Oakland Coliseum, Sacred Heart of San Francisco beat the Warriors, ending their season.

Sacred Heart went on to win the State Tournament, but the thrill of that upset, the thrill of that campaign, still bound Sara and Coach for life.

It was one of the fondest memories for both of them.

Coach loved the fact that Sara respected him so much. She thought so highly of his basketball analysis and recognized his absolute integrity when it came to the game. And on top of that, she appreciated his sense of humor.

Over the past few years they had shared a lot of laughter. She laughed at all his stories, some of the same ones over and over. Coach loved to tell stories and he loved it when he could find a captive audience like Sara. Sara loved to laugh, and so did Coach. Although it didn't come as easy for Coach as it used to. So many things had been lost these last few years, and one of them was his ability to laugh. To even smile.

Sara and Coach had grown together and became good friends over the years, but their relationship was still based on the fact that he had given her basketball, and this provided some of the most thrilling and exciting times of her life. Their relationship was once Coach-player, but over the years they had become good friends. Coach didn't have many people left in his life he could call friend anymore. He had isolated himself too much over the years in an effort to feel less vulnerable. Unconsciously, he had even sacrificed Joanie's companionship to avoid the possibility of future pain, disappointment, and grief. Slowly he had resorted to a solitary existence in an attempt to escape any more anguish and suffering. The cross he bore already was too heavy.

The fact that he was willing to risk Sara's friendship showed just how scared he really was. Or how far gone he was.

He cautiously told her about the dream.

He told her about the search and investigation of Travis. And he told her about the phone call.

When he finished they drove in silence for awhile.

They were now passing through Sacramento and its suburbs and beginning to climb into the foothills below Auburn. Rain had begun to fall, and the only sound seemed to be the windshield wipers trying to clear a path through the darkness. Sara had moved over to the fast lane and was passing the late night traffic as they climbed.
She was in a hurry now.
Coach tried to tell the story in a humorous way. A "can you believe that?" sort of way, but it didn't wash. Sara was a brilliant attorney. She could see right through it. She knew that he honestly believed that Lester Travis, possibly the best college basketball player in America, was Parker.
His son.

Wonder what she thinks of the brilliant coach now?

He tried to initiate a new conversation, but the shock wouldn't wear off.

He tried to make some small talk. Asked about the where-abouts of some of her teammates. Asked about some of the cases she was currently working on. But mostly they sat in silence, staring ahead into the darkness and the rain.

In Auburn they swung onto Highway 49 and headed north. They were now only thirty minutes from Empire.

The rain began to turn to snow as they climbed in elevation. It seemed to add to the dreariness and the sadness that had now set in between them.

She thinks I'm nuts. Sick. I must be nuts. I've opened Pandora's Box. Where's it going to go now? I can only imagine. She's got to be thinking about telling Joanie. Thinking I need help. Don't blame her. Don't blame her one bit.

The snow was beginning to stick when they pulled up Coach's driveway.

Before getting out of the car Coach had a request for Sara. "Sara, I'd appreciate it if you didn't say anything to Joanie. She thinks I'm nuts as it is."

"Oh, I won't Coach. Hey, don't worry about it," Sara was trying to be polite.

"Thanks, Sara. I had a great time," said Coach as he now stood in the darkness holding the passenger door open.

"Hey, it was fun Coach. Awesome games."

As Coach stood in the driveway and leaned in the open door of Sara's car to say his good-byes, he could sense she was anxious to get out of there.

"Good luck in Reno. Looks like you better carry your chains if you're going to get over the pass," said Coach.

"Sorta looks like it, Doesn't it? Won't be the first time," Sara said, trying to act cheerful again.

Let her go, you idiot. She wants to get outta here. Away from you. You old fool.

"Love you, Sara. Thanks again."

"Love you too, Coach. I'll be talking to you. Good night, Coach."

"Good night, Sara."

It was late. Early Friday morning in fact. But Coach dug a cigar out of a box he had stashed in the garage. He kept them hidden there despite the fact that he told Joanie he was quitting. He sat in a lawn chair in the backyard and smoked.

You are such a fool. Nothing worse than an old fool. Nothing worse. What have you done?

The snow landed on his face and melted with his tears.

CHAPTER TWELVE

MARCH 20, 2004

SATURDAY MORNING

Coach hated lying.

Hated it more than anything. He told Joanie a lie. Had to.

He told her he had a ticket to the game between Western Pacific and Indiana. He told her he bought it from a scalper Thursday night when Sara and he were leaving the game.

Only could get one ticket though. Paid only twenty dollars over face value. So he was heading back down to the Bay Area to go to the game.

She didn't seem to the mind all that much.

Didn't understand why anyone would want to go to a game by themselves, but once again, she was just glad to see he was getting out of the house.

It never dawned on her that it was the Western Pacific Pirates and Lester Travis that was playing.

Her primary concern was his late return and the possibility of more snow. In her mind, however, the initiative he was taking and the excitement he was showing was worth the risk.

She did want him to check the weather report when he left Oakland, and if the conditions were getting bad in the Sierras or if he was too tired to drive, he should just check into a motel for the night. She said he didn't have to get home just so he could get up at dawn and play with his computer.

Coach's primary concern was that while he was gone, Sara would call.

That would be disastrous.

Or worse yet. Joanie would get a threatening phone call from the security agency for Edward Travis. Putting himself in danger was one thing; putting her in danger was quite another. The last thing he wanted to do was hurt Joanie anymore.

His plan was to buy a scalper ticket at the game.

He had his doubts about actually being able to obtain a ticket. Coach read in the morning paper the game was a sell out. The internet said the same thing. He decided he was going anyway.

Around noon he swung by the bank and got a thousand dollars in cash. If he did find a ticket to buy it would surely be expensive. He was prepared to pay a lot.

A light rain began to fall as he drove out of town.

Get down to Oakland. Grab a bite to eat. Go to the Coliseum. Probably have to stand out in the rain. Find a ticket. Or find a bar. And watch it on TV.

He switched on his favorite Bay Area AM sports talk show and headed down Highway 49.

"What was the first movie Edward Travis produced?"

That was the sports trivia question on KNBR sports talk radio. The prize—two tickets to tonight's NCAA playoff game at the Oakland Coliseum.

Coach, of course, knew the answer.

He had become an authority on the history of Edward Travis. Could have written his biography.

The answer was *Nathan Shanaki.*

It was a film about the legendary mountain man who was raping and killing tourists in Yosemite Park. Nathan Shanaki was part myth, part legend. They never did find him. But supposedly, he was responsible for twelve unsolved rapes and murders.

The film never made it to theaters. It was released on video long after Travis' movie company was producing blockbusters. It was less than a "B" movie.

It was the first movie Travis and his film class buddies made their senior year at Western Pacific.

Practically no budget and no paid extras. The film crew made up most of the cast. Travis' roommate played the part of Nathan. And their college girlfriends played the naked screaming victims chopped up in their camping tents. It was full of nudity, fake blood and animal entrails. It was raunchy and violent. Very poor quality, shot with hand held cameras. The equipment used to film it was Western Pacific's, and there was a controversy about getting some of the money from the video donated back to the school. As far as Coach knew, that never happened.

The first movie Travis produced that made it to theaters was *Sons of the Beach.*

It was a movie about Malibu surf punks who attack, rape, rob, and kill members of LA street gangs. Once again, plenty of graphic violence and sex. Much more high tech than *Shanaki,* but it still was years away from any Oscar consideration for Travis.

The first caller to the talk show was positive it was *Sons of the Beach.*

The next caller tried *Tiajuana.*

That was the second film Travis managed to get in theaters. That one was about two college best friends who kidnap a young Mexican prostitute. Smuggle her back into the United States and use her to fulfill their sexual appetites. They keep her tied up in the bedroom of their apartment. Eventually they decide they have to get rid of her, but they can't decide how. Afraid of getting caught they decide to murder her. Chop her up and throw her in a dumpster.

But it turns out that one of the guys has fallen in love with her. So he offs his buddy instead. When the young prostitute is released by the remaining roommate and informed of his now deep affection for her, she kills him. She ends up chopping them both up and throwing them in a dumpster. She makes herself at home in their LA apartment and begins a new life. Plenty of R-rated mayhem. It was the first movie that made real money for Travis.

Coach pulled to the side of the road.

Boy, is this a long shot. I've never called into a talk show in my life.

He pulled out the cell phone and dialed the KNBR number.

What are the chances? Busy signal, right?

Someone answered.
At first Coach thought it must be a wrong number.
"Hello, KNBR. This is the Jack Smack Sports Attack."
Coach was completely taken by surprise, and the man who answered had to repeat himself.
"Hello, this is KNBR, the Jack Smack Sports Attack."
"I know the answer to today's sports trivia question," Coach finally blurted out.
"Hold on a minute. Could you please turn off your radio. We'll have an echo if you don't. Thanks."
Coach waited beside the freeway. A couple of minutes later Jack Smack himself was on the line.
"Hello, Jack Smack here. Who am I talking to?"
"Afternoon Jack. This is Pete Peterson."

Should have used an alias!

"And you've got the answer to today's trivia question, Pete Peterson?"

"Well I think I do," Coach said. "How about *Nathan Shanaki?*"

"Bingo! That's it. The horniest mountain man in history. Do you know who played the part of Nathan, Pete Peterson?"

"Christopher Goetz." Coach knew that one too.

"Wow, you are good. Christopher Goetz, who is now a pretty good movie maker in his own right. As a matter of fact he has just finished producing the big Civil War epic about Sherman's march through Atlanta. Soon to be released. This summer I guess. Well congratulations, Pete Peterson. You're on your way to see Travis' kid, Lester and his Western Pacific Pirate teammates take on the Indiana Hoosiers tonight at the Oakland Coliseum. Good job. Please stay on the line and we'll tell you where you can pick up your tickets."

"Thanks, Jack," Coach said, still amazed.

From the shoulder Coach cautiously pulled back on to the freeway. He was laughing. Rollicking. Passing drivers gave him strange looks.

DID THAT JUST HAPPEN? What a break! A lower level ticket waiting for me at Executive Will Call. What a break! Just so happens an Edward Travis trivia expert was listening to the show. Too bad I can't tell Joanie about it. The Travis thing is just too sensitive an area. Besides I told her I had a ticket. The big lie. I'll have to keep this story to myself. Too bad. It would have been a great story.

I can't believe it.

Well, on to Oakland. Find a rib joint. Celebrate my good fortune.

Unbelievable!

Unbelievable!

CHAPTER THIRTEEN

MARCH 20, 2004

SATURDAY NIGHT

REGIONAL FINAL

OAKLAND COLISEUM

Indiana played way over their heads.

Western Pacific struggled throughout against the determined upstart Hoosiers.

It looked as though Western Pacific thought the Hoosiers were going to roll over for them, and they weren't quite prepared mentally for as tough a battle as they were in for.

Maybe they read the morning papers. The odds makers had the Pirates a sixteen point favorite. But you could tell from the onset, it was not going to be a blowout. The Pirates had become everyone's new favorite to win the whole thing, but from the beginning of the game, Indiana looked very capable of pulling an upset.

Western Pacific could not get the easy transition baskets they were accustomed to.

No layups.

No break away dunks.

No showtime.

Indiana did a great job getting back on defense. Their primary concern was not to get second shots offensively, but to retreat quickly and lock the Pirates up with tough man to man half court defense. And Indiana played some of the most fundamentally tough team defense Coach had recently witnessed. In this day and age it was refreshing to see a such a hard working team defense.

The Pirate motion offense was not getting easy looks, and most of their offense was one on one as the shot clock was expiring.

Indiana's defense was rotating and getting help on all Western Pacific penetration. Smothering any passing or dribble invasion into the paint.

The Hoosiers took three charges in the first half.

To say the Pirate offense looked frustrated early on would be an understatement. They were forcing everything. Taking bad shot after bad shot. Leaners and fall aways.

Just two nights ago the Pirates looked unbeatable. Unstoppable. And now they looked completely out of sync.

The fortunate thing for Western Pacific was that Indiana had just as tough a time trying to score on them.

The Pirates team defense wasn't that sound, disciplined, or as tenacious as Indiana. They were just faster, bigger, and more athletic. They recovered quickly when they got beat, and they were able to block shots from behind. And because of their superior size, they got most of the rebounds.

The game was low scoring, and it stayed that way the entire 40 minutes.

It turned out to be one of the best college basketball games Coach, or anyone else in attendance for that matter, had ever had the privilege of witnessing.

Like the rest of the Pirates, Lester Travis was struggling too.

His defender was much smaller than he was, but was quick and stubborn. Adhesive. He was in Lester's face, bellying up and fighting through screens. You could tell he didn't have the help responsibility the rest of his teammates had. His job was to put the glove on Travis, and he was doing an exceptional job.

When Travis gave up the ball, his defender went right to a denial posture, and it was very difficult for Travis to get the ball back. It was making it almost impossible for Travis to run the offense. It was a great game plan and early on it was working to perfection.

At halftime the Pirates only had 10 field goals.

They were only 50% from the free-throw line, a horrid 7 for 14. They had 1 three point basket, which happened to be Lester Travis' only field goal. And it banked in.

However, the Hoosiers hadn't fared much better on the offensive end. They had only 8 field goals, but were 11 for 13 from the charity stripe.

The halftime score stood at Western Pacific 28—Indiana 27.

Most of what little offense there was came on tough inside play. Put-backs and tip-ins. It was very physical down low at the post, and there were very few open looks on the perimeter by either team. A couple of jump shots had gone down, and that was about it. The scoring was very unspectacular and lacked the crowd pleasing flair that the Pirates thrived on. Like most of the basketball of recent years, teams did not like to rely on 10 to 15 foot jump shots. The game today was dunks and treys followed by celebratory gestures for the benefit of the audience.

Coach's seat was a good one.

It was on the aisle behind the Pirate bench, approximately twenty rows up from the floor, the Western Pacific coaching staff right below him. Just a few rows below, and slightly to the left, sat Edward Travis, his wife Rebecca, and the rest of his posse. Coach assumed an aisle seat for Travis would be to risky and bothersome. Too many autograph seekers interrupting the game. He was insulated by associates, friends, whatever, and sat almost in the middle of his row of seats.

His wife was a rare addition.

She usually did not attend games. But at this level of media and public interest, she probably couldn't pass up the possibility of some major TV exposure.

She was definitely playing the cameras. Waving a Western Pacific pennant whenever she thought the camera might be looking for their reaction to something that was happening on the court.

Edward Travis looked annoyed, neither inviting or appreciating the attention his wife's antics were drawing from the televised coverage. He was much too anxious about the outcome of the game. Unlike his carefree, self-centered, exhibitionist wife, for him there was much too much at stake to be enjoying himself.

To Coach, Travis almost looked embarrassed by the way his wife continually flirted. Constantly trying to be the center of everyone's attention. Her looks and her outfit managed to get enough of that on their own. She was dressed more for a movie premiere than a basketball game. During the first half she managed to make contact with most of the celebrities that dotted the lower regions of the Coliseum. There were plenty of young actors, musicians and famous ex-jocks to flirt with.

Coach couldn't help but be amused by Edward Travis' annoyance and the distraction that his wife was causing. He could tell Travis was unable to devote his entire focus and concentration on the game, and it only added to his growing anxiety level.

This was a very important game to Edward Travis, one in which he had a huge investment.

And the outcome was very much in doubt.

The ends of the arena were filled with the student fans of both teams.

On the Indiana end of the floor, a sea of red. A huge throng of Indiana alumni and student body.

On the other end, the purple and gold Pirate faithful.

The cheering was raucous.

They traded amusing barbs, especially when the opposition was forced to shoot free-throws in the face of the other teams fans.

"Silver spoon" they chanted when Lester Travis had the ball or was shooting free-throws. Or "rape, murder, mayhem," in reference to his father's movie money makers.

It was brutal.

The Pirate fans chanted things like "No Jimmy, No gimmie" in reference to the movie "Hoosiers" now almost an ancient classic about a Hickory High Husker named Jimmy Chitwood who saves the day with a miraculous shot to win the Indiana State Tournament for the little town of Milan, Indiana. If there was a questionable call that Indiana Coach Byrun Marshall didn't agree with, they chanted "throw a chair" referring to a famous, and embarrassing, chair throwing incident executed many years before by ex-Indiana Head Coach Bobby Knight. It was one of many angry tirades that ultimately led to his dismissal after twenty-nine years as their Head Coach. Ironically, he happened to be court side doing TV color commentary for Fox Sports.

The place, of course, was packed. A sell out.
Standing room only. Tons of media.

On the way in Coach didn't see a single scalper trying to get rid of extra tickets. It made the fact that he was sitting there watching this game even more amazing.

The atmosphere was charged. More than tense. This wasn't an idle corporate crowd nonchalantly conversing, not really interested in the outcome or just hoping that sometime down the road they would impress someone by saying they had made the scene. This basketball game turned out to be something else. Something more.

To Coach, and to many other long time basketball aficionados, the match up between Indiana and Western Pacific ended up being more than just an early round match up between two college basketball teams in the NCAA tournament.

It had symbolism.

It was symbolic of two very contrasting basketball philosophies. The game in may ways represented the changes in coaching principles. Indiana, of course, represented the "old school." Western Pacific was the emerging "new world" leadership. The "my way or the highway" as opposed to "we're all in this together," theory of coaching. A rigid system versus flexibility. Coach's regulations versus player's rule.

And the fact that both these teams understood exactly what they were, who they were, and the fact that they were both very proud of it, made the contest even more compelling.

Indiana represented the old, conservative and vanishing belief in tough half court man to man defense with ball control offense. The Hoosiers were still champions of the old status quo.

Western Pacific, on the other hand, were the radical revolutionists. Believing in bushwhacking bedlam. Full court press. Full court offense.

It was tradition versus new wave.

These two teams were not just separated by geography either. There were other differences. If you looked closer, you could find other fascinating dissimilarities.

This wasn't just Indiana versus Western Pacific! No way.

It was rural hick versus city slick. Bebop versus hip hop. It was 7 to 4 and hope for some overtime hours versus "slept till noon." Meat and Potatoes versus "Lets have lunch." Farm house and pick up trucks versus mansions and Mercedes. Ponds versus pools. Shoveling snow versus surf and sun.

If you were in attendance, an idle spectator, neutral at best, you were forced to pick a side. Uninvolved was not allowed. The whole polarization of America itself was brought to the forefront and it was time you declared your loyalty.

Civil War was breaking out.

In reality, of course, only a Sweet Sixteen birth was on the line. A trip to the America West Arena in Phoenix, and a chance to take a shot at getting to the Final Four in San Antonio.

The Pirates were only holding a 1 point lead in a game many felt would be a cake walk for them. A mere formality, on the way to the Final Four.

The Hoosier players and fans, who had their doubts, that really didn't believe this was their year, were now pumped for an upset, and the long shot chance of playing for the National Championship once again. An unlikely opportunity to add to their colorful history. A Hoosier team that could play with reckless abandon, with a nothing to lose attitude, was now a very dangerous one.

The Pirates were getting the test of their lives, and only in the second round. Last year it was the Pirates that surprised many. They had cruised through the first two rounds. A birth in the Sweet Sixteen this year was a given by most sportswriters.

But the Pirates looked very human tonight. Ordinary.

The Cinderella slipper was on the other team's foot. This game now loomed as the possible upset of the tournament.

Maybe one of the biggest upsets in the whole history of the tournament. It would certainly rank way up there.

Many of the Pirate devoted were starting to recall the shocking collapse against the University of Wisconsin-Green Bay some years before. When the Pirates had a chance of actually winning a game in the tournament, something in their short history they had never done before. Only Dick Bennett and his UW-GB Phoenix embarrassed them with a 20 point defeat. In the first round! A lower seed! Although this was the second round, they were now a tremendous favorite. The thought of having their name being attached to two of the biggest shockers in the history of the tournament was too much to even think about.

But it was obvious in the first half.
The Pirates were playing not to lose.
And the Hoosiers were playing to win.

And the second half turned out to be more of the same.
The potential of a Pirate run never materialized.

At the ten-minute mark, the Western Pacific lead did get to five.
With the game tied, Travis made a great fastbreak feed to a streaking teammate who executed a two handed dunk. On the following possession Indiana turned the ball over, and Travis hit a pull-up three at the top of the key.
Indiana called a time-out.
The Pirate fans were going crazy.
Even Edward Travis looked a little relieved. Everyone thought that this was finally the run they needed to put the Hoosiers away.
Finally the knockout had come.
But on the very first possession after the time-out, Indiana executed a great play and hit a three of its own. The lead dropped back to two, and it was the Indiana supporters' turn to breath a sigh of relief.
The game from there to the final buzzer was a one possession game. Each team's fans agonizing over a failed attempt to score or an opportunity to capitalize on the other team's futility.

In the last five minutes the lead changed hands seven times. They were tied six times.

Indiana refused to go away.
Outmanned but never out maneuvered.
They refused to get rattled by the Pirate press. Much too patient. Their defense was just too solid, too fundamentally sound to allow any driving lanes. There were no cracks or seams. No outside open looks. The Pirates were struggling to remain patient and struggling to execute any half court offense. They continued to appear baffled. Frustrated and exasperated.

Down the stretch every possession became more and more excruciating in its importance.
Both combatants fighting to stave off tournament elimination.

Survive!

Advance!

Both offenses resolute and agonizingly bent on scoring what could be the game winning basket each and every time down the court.

Coach loved it. This was basketball. Traditional. Old guard. The old ways. Handed down throughout the generations. Where defense actually mattered. Where defense could be appreciated. Defense wins. Basketball only an old-time purist could understand.

Points were so extremely hard to come by; each time a team would finally score, the fans celebrated as if that basket was the one that won the game.
It was physical. It wasn't so much that the refs were letting them play as much as they were unable to call everything

without literally having to stop the game with every possession.

Hand-to-hand combat.

Not just another skirmish. Not just another battle over a
long campaign. It was much more than that. To the players and
fans it was becoming life or death.
You could see it on their faces.
There was no in-between. They played and cheered as if
their lives were literally at stake.
If they were a part of winning no other game the rest of
their lives, it didn't matter. This one victory would suffice.
It simply had to be won.
There were no other options.
The losers were coming home on their shields. The winners
would march in victoriously and occupy the homeland of their
minds forever. No in between. Do. Or die trying.

Up until now there were no great players in this game. No
flashy five star generals leading their comrades to glory. There
were only tired, exhausted, battle weary grunts, refusing to
surrender. Never knowing when the next shell might be the
one that ends their life. Never knowing when fatigue would
finally zap them of the last remnant of courage and their will to
live.

At the time neither team realized that they were participating in a game that would remain a classic. An encounter that
would be talked about and rehashed for many years to come. A
contest whose highlights would be played over and over along
with many of the great moments in the tournament history. A
rivalry created that would endure for decades.
The pressure that was produced by this performance surpassed any match-up that materialized in the tournament in
recent memory.

Let alone it was happening in the second round!

This game would end up definitely stealing this year's show.

The student fans who were so delirious and fun loving in the first half were now frozen, motionless, much too frightened to do anything else except bite their lips or chew on their fingers.

The pressure hung on them like a Texas humidity and they grew paralyzed as if they themselves held the ball in their own hands with the game on the line.

They were like transfixed boxing fans who came to a fight to have fun and watch a physical and brutal battle, only to have it end with the death of one of the participants. And were now forced to leave feeling guilty and ashamed because moments before they were urging the contestants on.

The fans in the Coliseum who were only moments earlier eating hot-dogs and nachos, laughing and cheering, gradually began to grow silent, hoping and praying for an end to the violence. An end to the carnage.

With twenty-three seconds left, Western Pacific had the ball.

Indiana had just converted one of two free-throws by their big man to break a tie and go up by 1.

The Pirates dribbled the ball to half court and called a time-out. Coach Schmidt, the Western Pacific Head Coach, drew up an inbound play.

From where Coach was sitting in the stands he could see that it took a while for Schmidt to calm down his troops. They were all trying to offer their opinions. He finally got them quiet and diagrammed what he thought could be their game winner.

When the ball was inbounded, Coach was not quite sure what the play was supposed to be. Travis did end up with the ball but after he received it, his teammates stopped moving. No screens.

Travis tried to drive to the basket.

And once again the Hoosiers collapsed and closed off the lane. Travis dished the ball to his power forward who took it hard to the rim.

He failed to score but was fouled by Indiana. Two free-throws.

Now it was the Pirate's turn on the free-throw line with the game in the balance.

Fifteen seconds.

Indiana called a time-out to freeze the shooter.

When the teams returned, the Pirate player calmly made the first one.

Game tied.

He missed the second one and Indiana rebounded, quickly outletted, and pushed it to half court. They called their last time-out.

Twelve seconds.

The opposing coaches huddled with their assistants before addressing their squads.

The five Western Pacific players who were on the floor when the time-out was called sat down in chairs with their backs to the crowd. Travis sat in the middle. The reserves stood and faced them. All had their heads down quietly waiting for their coach to enter the huddle. Their quiet demeanor was a marked contrast from the chaos of their last time-out. Bravado had been replaced with doubt. Disbelief.

Coach Peterson stared down at Lester Travis as a manager handed him a yellow water bottle. His name had been written on the bottle with a black magic marker-TRAVIS. Instead of drinking the contents through the spout, he popped the top off and took a long drink before capping it and handing it back to the manager.

The Pirates looked exhausted. Too tired, too tense to speak to each other.

Coach Schmidt kneeled down in front of the sitting Pirate players and gave them their final instructions. The players stood up, put their hands in the circle and in unison yelled "TEAMWORK" before taking the floor.

With the game tied, it was obvious what Indiana's strategy would be. Run the clock down and take a shot at the buzzer to win the game.

Western Pacific, of course, had to be careful not to foul. Indiana was in the bonus.

The Hoosiers set up their play.

Travis's man took the ball from the referee. He would be the inbounder.

The two Indiana posts set a double screen at the free-throw line for their shooting guard who came from down low under the net. He raced to the top of the key and received the ball on the inbound pass from Travis' man. He immediately returned the pass to the point guard and they spread the floor.

10-9-8. . .

Screen on ball by the shooting guard-it was a pick and roll! Indiana never screened on the ball!

Their motion offense almost always consisted of passing and screening away.

Western Pacific always played the pick and roll aggressively.

Even though they hadn't talked about the possibility of Indiana trying to execute such a play, they did what they normally do. Instinctively. They double teamed the ball, and relied on their defensive rotation to take away the roller.

Travis and his teammate trapped the dribbler. He pulled up his dribble and attempted to pass over the top of the trap to the shooting guard rolling to the basket. He was wide open!

The pass, however, was deflected.

It squirted toward Western Pacific's basket, and the three players gave chase. Lester, his teammate, and the Indiana guard.

7-6-5 . . .

At the top of the key, on the Pirate end of the floor, Travis' teammate and the Indiana guard tangled and went to the floor.

The ball continued to roll past the free-throw line.

4-3-2. . .

Travis hurdled the two players on the floor. Slapped the ball once and grabbed the bounce with two hands.
He rose from the floor and executed a dramatic two-handed dunk.

He was swinging from the rim when the horn sounded.

When Coach ever looked back and thought about that particular play, he remembered there being a second, or even seconds, when the entire arena was silent. A tree fell in the forest, and there was no one around. It was if it took awhile for everyone to realize just what had happened. "Did that really just happen?" They looked at Lester Travis swinging on the rim, then at the scoreboard, back at the floor, at each other. Only then did it seem to sink in.
Then suddenly it was as if someone turned on a stereo, not knowing that when it had been turned off previously, the volume had been left turned all the way to the max. . . .
It got loud!
Unrestrained. Rowdy. Wild and unruly!

The Western Pacific bench emptied and tried to dog pile with the players on the floor. The Pirate coaching staff was running with them, waving their arms in the air and shouting along with the players. Most of the stands began to pour onto the floor.

Not just the Western Pacific fans, but the Indiana fans also.

The red-shirted Hoosier fans could be seen slapping the Pirate players on the back and helping the Western Pacific fans lift the players on their shoulders. Not just the Pirate players, but the Hoosiers as well.

Travis was hoisted up by such a group of students, red clad kids, along with the purple and gold. He was paraded around the floor, screaming and thrusting his fist into the air.

The ensuing riot recognized the incredible effort by both teams, and the unbelievable finish that they all shared.

They commemorated the fact that, along with the players, they had survived this battle of attrition with their dignity, for the most part, still in tact. Exuberant over the fact that the passion and loyal enthusiasm they loved to display at sporting events had not become casualties during the bloody conflict.

They seemed so relieved that the fanaticism and energy they had expended had somehow now been justified. And the misgivings and consternation they had earlier about their over-all self worth were suddenly erased by an incredible finish to a college basketball game. Self doubts and impending shame were replaced with pride and a pure sense of joy which they now collectively shared down on the Coliseum floor.

When the Pirates stole the ball, Coach, like everyone else, stood up.

To get a better view he stepped into the aisle adjacent to his seat. When the buzzer sounded he was swept down the aisle toward the floor by blitzed patrons trying to get a better look or to get on the floor itself to join the chaos. He found himself standing along side the Western Pacific bench. He glanced down to where the Pirate manager sat behind the players' chairs and saw a rack of the players water bottles. There was Lester Travis' water bottle. The one Coach had seen earlier. His name clearly written in large black letters down the side.

The manager must be out on the floor.

He leaned down and grabbed it.
Impulsively.
It was still half full.
He quickly slid it under his arm inside of his overcoat.
It surprised him a little that no one took any notice. But all eyes were on the festivities on the floor.

Coach slowly backed his way up the steps, lightly clapping while protecting the bottle he held under his arm inside of his coat. He was completely undetected, and when he reached the row where his seat had been, he turned and scrambled up the aisle to the exit.

With the thunderous sounds of the celebration still echoing behind him, Coach left the arena.

CHAPTER FOURTEEN

MARCH 26, 2004

FRIDAY

FLIGHT TO PHOENIX

Last Monday Coach carefully wrapped the water bottle and with the help of Federal Express, sent it overnight to Sara Rick.

He enclosed a short explanation along with a lock of his own hair.

That was to be the end of it. Have it DNA tested. Maybe fingerprinted.

Done. Done deal.

Science. Modern medicine. That would put and end to all of this nonsense.

He figured that after Sara received the bottle, she probably could no longer keep it a secret from Joanie. She would be too alarmed, too worried not to tell Joanie that he actually believed Lester Travis was their son, Parker.

And Joanie was going to hit the roof.

He was prepared to fall back on the water bottle being the final thing that he would do.

The water bottle was it.

No more. Done. Done deal. Irrefutable truth. One way or the other.

*I'm not even sure they can run tests with the water bottle.
Probably can't. Doesn't matter. Enough is enough. Have to put an end
to all of this. Get a life, Peterson. Get a life.*

He decided he would no longer pursue Edward Travis. No
more research. No more investigation. No more secret agent.
He would painstakingly reassure Joanie. It was over. Over. And
after awhile he hoped time would put this all behind them.

He was wrong.
Sara didn't call Joanie.

And for a few days their life was back to normal.
Until Thursday.

Then Coach announced he was going to Phoenix.

Coach called an ex-player of his, Julie McCauley, who was
now living in the Phoenix area, and she gave him the name and
number of an out-of-the-way little motel that still might have a
vacancy. In was even reasonably close to the America West
Arena where the games were to be played.
She was right. They had one room left. Single. Smoking.
Perfect.
So Coach reserved it.
Julie McCauley was a reserve on Coach's State Championship team. When she graduated from Brigham Young University, where she walked on and made the basketball team, she
came back home and helped out by coaching the Junior Varsity.
Over the years she had developed into a very accomplished role
player at BYU, and she developed into even a better coach.
During spring break after her second season as the JV
coach, she vacationed in the Caribbean. There she met a young
businessman from Phoenix. They fell in love and got married
that summer.

Now they had two children, and she was teaching and coaching at a middle school in a Phoenix suburb. Over the last few years they only kept track of each other through family, friends, and ex-teammates.

She was surprised but happy to hear from him.

Coach had to turn down her persistent offer that he stay at her house.

He also had to turn down her offer to pick him up at the airport. He said he wanted to rent a car so he could have the freedom of seeing the local sights during the weekend. Of course, he was already back to secret mission mode, and there was no way he was going to share what he was really planning.

Involving Sara Rick had been risky and embarrassing enough. He told Julie he would call when he got settled in and they could get together for a lunch or maybe dinner.

He had to tell yet another lie.

He told Joanie he had a ticket to the game.

The lies were piling up now. They were becoming easier and they were coming with less guilt. He had become a liar, one of the things he hated the most.

The lies poured out on Thursday when Joanie grew suspicious. Joanie caught on to what was happening.

"It's Western Pacific isn't it, Pete? The team with the Travis kid?" Joanie asked.

"They're a great team Joanie, and it turns out I just love watching them play," Coach lied. Another little white lie to hide his real intentions.

"You're stalking Travis. There's laws, Pete. You could go to jail. Worse yet. Get yourself killed."

"Honey, Julie called. She had tickets. Southwest Airlines. $129. Round trip. A Holiday Inn special. $69."

All lies.

There were no tickets.

The flight was $479. He put it on his secret credit card. The motel was $179 a night. He put that on his secret credit card also.

A phone call from Sara would have blown his cover. It would confirm just how far gone he was, just how pathetic he was becoming.

Hopefully Sara won't call until Friday. By that time I'll be on the plane. Then it won't matter. If she calls during the weekend, that won't matter either. I'll be in Phoenix. I'll be gone. When I return, I'll beg forgiveness. What's Joanie going to do? She'll get over it.

Early Friday morning he drove to Sacramento and boarded the plane.

He felt he would have plenty of time when he reached Phoenix to rent a car, check in at the motel, and then drive on over to the Arena and try to score a ticket. He still had his wad of money from last weekend.

This is crazy. But it's kind of exciting. Secret agent. But you know, it's just a basketball game. Right? Just a basketball game. It really doesn't need to be anything more than that. It's OK. It's all right. People do these things you know. It's just a game.

It was overcast in Sacramento. Not foggy like it is so much of the time during the spring months. There were no delays and the plane left on time.

Once they were airborne the stewardess came around to offer refreshments.

Coach sat at a window seat above the wing. Next to him sat a couple who conversed to each other in Spanish. They seemed uninterested or unable to strike up a conversation with him, and that suited Coach just fine.

The couple ordered juice. When it was his turn to order he had the sudden urge to order alcohol.

A beer.

It took Coach by surprise.

He hadn't had the urge to drink alcohol in some time. Hadn't even thought about it recently. The urges came and went over the last few decades but Coach hadn't once, not even once, conceded to the desire. He still thought of taking a drink, one single drink, as committing suicide. Poison.

One drink.

Suicide.

Didn't even drink wine at the communion service in church.

It might take longer than blowing your brains out or slashing your wrists, but it would lead to the same thing-Death. Over the years no matter how despondent he got, no matter how confused or frustrated, he still didn't consider drinking again as an option. To end it all. To live and die as a drunk. That was no longer an option. And it hadn't been for years.

Now, out of nowhere, it crept in.

Maybe that's the only way I get out of this. Fall off the wagon. Blame it on the booze. It's been so long. Maybe I'm not an alcoholic anymore. That would be something. To find out after all these years I could have a beer and not go off the deep end. The shrink back in college was right. It was depression. Just depression. Insecurity. You could have handled that. Genetically doomed. Yeah right!

Jokes on you, Peterson!

After all these years.

You could have killed some of the pain. Maybe got a little more sleep. Relieved a little of the stress. But noooo. Instead you bought all that crap about having a disease.

Jokes on you, stupid!

Did I really think I was never going to drink again anyway?

"What can I get for you, sir?"

Coach looked up at the stewardess, mouth agape, not responding.

She asked him again. "Can I get you anything, sir? Something to drink?"

This time Coach blurted something out. "Orange juice. Orange juice," he repeated a second time a little louder. "Thank You. Thank you."

Maybe I'll buy a six pack in Phoenix. Wait until I get to the motel tonight. Do a little experiment. If I can't buy a ticket I'll have to watch the game in my motel. I could buy a six pack. Pound a few beers. Who'd know?

He took a sip on his orange juice and placed it back on his tray. He leaned his seat back and closed his eyes. A mild version of one of his recent panic attacks swept through.

This is crazy! This is crazy! Joanie is right. Joanie is always right. I'm nuts! I need help!
Turn the plane around!
Turn it around!
Crash! The plane is going to crash!
I wish it would crash. That would put an end to this.
I'll turn around in Phoenix. Get right back on a plane and go home. I'll tell Joanie my flight was canceled.
Go home. Where it's safe. Safe. I can hide away. Hide away.
It's just a game. It's just a game. You can go to a basketball game. Nothing wrong with that. People go to games everyday for crying out loud. It's just a game. Just a game. Live a little, will you? Live a little.

The attack passed and he fell into a deep sleep. It was one of those deep and sudden slumbers where the dreams come early.

He dreamt he was on the beach. The beach at the Wai Lai Resort in Maui.

Joanie and Coach took Parker, Michelle, and Michelle's best friend, Becky, to the resort two summers in a row back when Parker was two, and then again when he was three.

Parker loved the beach so much.

One big sand box.

Coach and Parker had spent hours practically from the time they got up until sunset, building sand castles and playing in the surf. They built their fortresses just close enough to the water so eventually a wave would wash over their citadels, and the towers and tunnels they had created would melt back into the beach swallowed up by the sea. The plastic shovels and buckets would be immediately put back to work to build another.

Parker would occasionally take breaks from building to chase the waves, charging at a subsiding wave as it withdrew back toward the sea, and then hurriedly retreating to the safety of the beach as the counterattack came rolling in. Parker would be laughing during the whole process, and Coach would sit with a smile on his face marveling at the endless uninhibited display of spirit and stamina.

Even when the surf scored a knockdown, Parker would jump back up giggling hysterically, ready to resume the bout.

He eventually would have everyone's attention along that stretch of the beach, and Parker's antics would put a smile on their faces. The people walking by with their snorkeling equipment would laugh with Parker as they carefully avoided him rushing in and out of the ocean. The vacationers who positioned themselves on the beach daily, like Coach and Parker, would now know Parker by name and would make a point to say hi to him. He was so carefree. So happy. Coach was so proud.

They played for hours, sometimes until the sun was beginning to touch the horizon.

Then they would gather up their plastic construction equipment and head up to the pool to meet Joanie, Michelle, and Becky. The three of them preferred hanging out at the pool that overlooked the Wai Lai beach.

Michelle and Becky would then play in the pool with Parker until the sun went down. They would all then head up to the condominium, shower, and maybe head for Lahaina for dinner. By the time they got back Parker would be asleep in his car seat to get his rest and become re-energized and revitalized for the next day's beach assault.

Those two summer vacations had been a slice of heaven. Paradise. And although it was an extravagant and expensive vacation for their family budget, Joanie and Coach agreed, it was worth every penny.

Coach woke to the sound of the pilot's announcement that they were beginning their descent into Phoenix and the stewardesses should prepare for a landing.

His eyes were wet. So were his cheeks.

He realized he had been crying. Crying in his sleep.

His pants were wet too.

During his dream he had bumped his tray and spilt his orange juice. It ran all over his tray and down onto his lap. He looked down at the mess and didn't quite know what to do. The couple next to him were trying not to stare down at the mess too.

Too bad, huh? You got stuck next to the pathetic old man who made a mess all over himself. And cries in his sleep. I should be embarrassed. Sorry. Too old for that.

Luckily a passing flight attendant had noticed the mess and promptly showed up with a towel. Because of his window position he was forced to clean most of it up himself. The crotch of his khaki trousers were soaked.

The flight attendant returned. "Can I get you anything else? Are you OK now?"

"Oh yeah, I'm fine. I could use a dry pair of pants. Hopefully it was just orange juice." He began to laugh.

It is rather pathetic, but whatever happened to laughing at yourself?

His dream helped recall a wonderful memory, one that had turned a little somber through the years. But still one that remained one of his all time Parker favorites.

He had slept almost the entire flight. Slept deeply. He awoke refreshed. His sense of adventure renewed.

His trusty overcoat was above him in the storage compartment. He probably didn't need it in Phoenix, but now it could be employed to conceal his accident. It would help get him through the airport and to the car rental counter without drawing too much attention. He would just get to his motel and change before heading over to the arena to find a ticket.

Got to get a ticket.
Got to see this game.
Show some hustle, Peterson!
Some determination!
This will be fun. This should be fun.
An adventure.
Some great basketball. Western Pacific versus Kansas. Arizona versus Oklahoma.
This'll be great.
No harm here.
Just basketball.
Well, maybe it's a little more than that.

My kid is playing.

CHAPTER FIFTEEN

MARCH 26, 2004

FRIDAY NIGHT

AMERICA WEST ARENA

PHOENIX

Coach got ripped off.

He was so worried he wouldn't get a ticket he bought the very first one offered to him. He paid four hundred dollars.

Boy, did they see me coming, or what? An old geezer. Old man in an overcoat! "Who wants him? Easy money here!"

He purchased the ticket near the gate entering the parking lot and the closer he got to the arena, the more ticket scalpers there were.

Most of them were just regular guys trying to unload an extra ticket and selling it for face value. They were also better seats than the one he purchased. His seat turned out to be four rows from the top. Four rows from where the wall met the ceiling. Although they were calling it a sell-out, there were empty seats all around him. If those seats had been sold, the occupants must have chosen some other vantage point: the bar, an entrance way, at home on the couch, or their motel room, where Coach was beginning to wonder if he wouldn't have been better off.

Maybe I should have bought another ticket? Probably get ripped off again. Get a counterfeit. And then I'd have to sell my four hundred dollar special. Get arrested for scalping. Hey, look on the bright side. I'm here. I made it. I'm in.

So Coach sat down with his large bucket of popcorn and big-gulp diet cola and watched Arizona and Oklahoma warm up.

Oklahoma was a big team.

They were seven-foot, six-ten, six-nine, in the front court. Their shooting guard was six-seven.

They were known for using a variety of full court zone presses, which they changed depending on how they scored. If they scored from inside, they jumped into a 1-2-1-1 diamond press; if they scored from the outside, they used a 2-2-1 dog press. When they got to their spots after they scored and got their arms out and hands up, they presented problems for most teams. Tremendous wing spans. They deflected a lot of balls in the passing lanes.

Arizona was young.

But very athletic. They started two freshmen and three sophomores. They had become the Cinderella team of the tournament, a role that Indiana would have challenged them for if they had succeeded in knocking off Western Pacific. Arizona had managed to pull two upsets in Dallas. They beat Santa Clara in the first round, and then pulled a shocker over the tenth ranked Arkansas Razorbacks.

The Oklahoma Sooners, on the other hand, were no Cinderella story. Far from it. They were the number two seed in the West behind Western Pacific.

Many sportswriters had labeled the Sooners the dark horse of the tournament. And their play so far in the tournament had justified that classification. They came into the tournament ranked eighth in the nation and made short work of Southwest

Missouri State and DePaul in the first two rounds of the tournament. The odds makers were now predicting a huge match-up in the Western Finals between fourth ranked Western Pacific and Oklahoma on Sunday.

That possible encounter would determine who would then represent the Western Region and pack their bags for San Antonio.

It was men against boys.

Arizona's tournament run was over.

Oklahoma dominated from the opening tip.

Too big. Too strong. Too much.

The Sooners had twelve dunks off of offensive rebounds. Even with a widening margin, Oklahoma showed a lot of discipline and patience in their half court offense. They swung the ball until they were able to get it into their big men, and then they finished with powerful post moves. Many of those were resounding two handed flushes. The Sooners consistently got the ball close to the basket and ended up shooting 76% from the field.

Their presses slowed down Arizona in transition just enough so everyone could get back, and then forced Arizona to launch three-point bombs. Every Arizona Wildcat miss, which were way too many, resulted in what seemed like a Sooner rebound. Oklahoma would then methodically set up their patient half court pummeling from the post.

Oklahoma's lead reached 25 with 8 minutes to go.

At that point the Wildcats surrendered and began to empty their bench.

Game over.

Not very exciting. But impressive. Few teams won so easily in the third round.

Now if Western Pacific took care of business, the battle for the Final Four spot from the West would become very intriguing.

Comparative scores? Western Pacific had beaten Arizona twice in the Pac-Twelve Conference. They beat them by twenty at home and by ten in Tucson. However, that was over a month ago before the Wildcats started to come of age, but in the two previous match-ups the Pirates were never pushed by the Cats.

Western Pacific did take care of business.

Kansas played hard and with determination, but the Pirates were hitting on all cylinders. Once again it was obvious Western Pacific was capable of playing as well as the three teams ranked above them. Duke, Kentucky and Purdue had not been tested in the tournament yet, but when Western Pacific put it together, they were very impressive. Their play against the Kansas Jayhawks once again had people thinking they could go all the way. Forget about the Indiana game, that was a fluke. Oklahoma was definitely going to be a test, but WPU was not a pretender. Their performance had succeeded in reestablishing themselves as a legitimate contender.

The Western Pacific press wreaked havoc on Kansas in the first half.

It fueled spurts of 10, and then 8 unanswered points. It put the Jayhawks in a hole early and they couldn't dig themselves out.

Lester Travis was 5 for 7 from the three-point line, many of them pull-ups off the break. Maybe it had something to do with the fact that Western Pacific had the scare of their lives in the last round, because from the opening tip they played with a renewed sense of desperation.

At times Kansas looked awestruck.

Happy to be there. Excited. But any thoughts of actually winning the game were erased early. By the time they realized they were in a game, it was too late.

At half time Western Pacific led 48-22.

The second half was more of the same.

Travis had 27 points when he came out at the four minute mark. The reserves for both teams finally brought the game to a sloppy ending.

Pirate blowout.

The final score was 91-53.

The great eight was now set, and it included some engaging match-ups.

Six of the final eight teams started the tournament ranked in the top ten. There was a mix of consistently strong squads led by coaches who had been at the helm for some time and there were some up and coming contingents led by young, innovative and dynamic coaches.

There was also an interesting collection of styles represented. Some teams, like Western Pacific, relied on the press and a run-and-gun fastbreak offense. Other teams liked to slow it down, set it up, and run an assortment of plays and sets at you.

Certain teams preferred speed and athleticism. Other teams loved size, strength and pounding it inside.

One thing they did all have in common; they all possessed the talent, depth, and coaching needed to win it all. On Saturday for the Eastern Region Championship, Duke would play Kentucky. In the South it would be Florida versus North Carolina. On Sunday in the Midwest it would be Purdue and Marquette and in the West, Oklahoma would square off with Western Pacific.

All eight were battling for a Final Four berth and a trip to the Alamodome in San Antonio.

When Coach went to leave the arena, he realized he forgot to make a mental record of where he parked his rental car.

To further complicate matters, he exited on the opposite side of the fieldhouse from where he had entered. When Coach drove into the parking lot, it was still daylight. Now it was dark, and he had a difficult time trying to get his bearings.

Great! This is going to be tricky. Real tricky. "Half-timers disease" old man? You were in such a big hurry! I don't even remember exactly what my rental looked like. Blue? Mid-sized? Was it a Ford? I know I parked a long way from the entrance. But where?

After the third lap around the lot, he realized it was hopeless. He meandered back to the steps of the entrance he vaguely remembered entering and decided to wait until the lot emptied.

Have to camp awhile. Six pack's gonna have to wait.

At least it was a pleasant evening.

A rare thunderstorm had passed through Phoenix while the games were being played. Although it was brief, it dumped quite a bit of rain, leaving some pretty good sized puddles around the parking lot. The temperature, however, was mild and even though it was getting late, it was still in the low sixties.

After thirty or forty minutes of hanging out, Coach noticed a small crowd beginning to form around the corner from where he was sitting.

A charter bus was pulled up above a lower entrance ramp. Coach figured it was probably there to pick up one of the basketball teams and take them to their hotel. The crowd that was forming looked like family, friends, and fans of one of the teams. Eventually the cheerleaders emerged from the doors behind Coach to join the waiting crowd.

It was the Pirate cheerleaders.

Coach realized it was the WPU Pirates who would be emerging from the locker room to get on the bus. Arena security was quickly erecting a portable metal fence to provide a barrier for the players to walk from the door of the security exit up the ramp to the bus.

Coach got up and decided to walk over and join the throng of well wishers.

Suddenly he recognized Edward Travis.

He was standing by the metal barrier in a group of people closest to the bus. He was surrounded by a group of mostly men.

Associates? Maybe some other dads? Bodyguards?

Two of the men standing next to Travis occasionally spoke with him but remained very vigilante. As they talked to Travis, or each other, they never took their eyes off the assembling crowd.

Coach found a spot about two to three deep near the rail. He was only roughly twenty-five feet from the bus and where Edward Travis was standing.

This is great. I'm going to get to see the team emerge. Get to see Parker in streets. Up close. Maybe he'll see me. Something might click.

After a few minutes of waiting he noticed the two men standing next to Travis looking in his direction.

Are they looking at me? They're looking over here. At me?

They were talking to each other both facing Coach's direction. Looking like, what seemed to be, right at him.

Don't stare at them, you idiot! Look casual. Like you belong here. Like you know somebody.

Coach looked away. Tried to look like he was minding his own business. Out of the corner of his eye he saw one of them now pointing in his direction. The other man nodded slowly and began to walk toward Coach.

Is he heading for me? No way! He's coming this way! Everyone else out here is with someone. In a group. You're the only one who looks suspicious. Here he comes!

Coach froze. His pulse instantly began to accelerate. He stood looking away now, toward the locker room doors. But in the corner of his eye he could still see the man approaching, feel him getting closer. He was heading right for Coach.

"Excuse me, sir," the stranger said as he approached.
Coach turned to look at the man now standing next to him.

He recognized the voice immediately.

"Are you a relative of one of the players? Of a Pirate? You look so familiar," he asked.
"No," Coach casually replied. Trying his hardest to remain calm. "Just a fan."
"Wait a minute," the bodyguard started.
He was a large man. Burley. A gorilla. Maybe in his late twenties, early thirties at the most, Coach thought. A weight lifter. He more than filled up his trench coat. He looked like he was born too late for it. Not everyone can wear a trench coat or fit in one for that matter. He had a large square head, no neck, that sat on broad shoulders, and his flat top hair cut made his head look enormous and even more menacing. He had a thick unkempt mustache glistening with salvia. His clothes were high quality but when you dress up an ape, it's still a primate.
"I know I've seen you before. You go to a lot of these games? Right? You look so familiar. We must have met at one of these games before."
"No, I don't think so." Coach now turned and looked back toward the concourse and the security exit where the players would soon be emerging.

Hurry up! If the team would start to get out here this guy might get off my back. I can't just walk away now, he'll be too suspicious. Maybe even follow me.

"Just a fan, huh? Well, where are you from? Are you from

around here? Your voice is so familiar," the thug continued his interrogation.

"I'm just a fan. A basketball fan. From California." Coach tried to put a little attitude in his response now.

When he turned to respond he could see the other man standing back by Travis looking in their direction. He now held a small microphone in his hand. Coach looked back at the bodyguard standing next to him and now noticed the ear plug. His interrogator was listening to something the other man was telling him.

"Wait a minute! You're not just a fan. You're old man Peterson. The snoop. We talked on the phone not too long ago. Didn't we? Didn't we?" the interrogator asked as he now stepped a little closer.

He began to squeeze between Coach and the portable fence until he was almost chest to chest with him.

"I think we better get out of here, Peterson," the bodyguard spoke low, whispered, so nobody standing nearby could hear him, but it was still a command spoken through somewhat clenched teeth.

He put his hand in his pocket and began to gently nudge Coach with his shoulder, moving him backward, away from the crowd of people at the fence.

Did he have a gun? A gun in his pocket? Is this really happening? Is this for real? Come on. A gun?

"We don't want to make a scene here. We need a little space. Somewhere we can talk." The ape continued to push Coach with his shoulder and his chest but was forcing a smile while continuing to survey the scene. When Coach turned his back to the crowd, the bodyguard reached up and grabbed onto one of his arms.

Coach wasn't offering much, if any, resistance. He was too frightened for any heroics. He was letting himself be led away from the assemblage.

What the heck. This is crazy. I'm not doing anything. Do some-thing! Say something! Resist. Should I make a scene? Say something!

"Hey, you know what? I'm not bothering you. I'm not bothering anyone. So what is the problem?" Coach was too apprehensive to offer any physical resistance to the hard charg-ing gorilla, so he thought he'd try to muster some verbal resistance. Voice some kind of objection. Consider getting loud. Call attention to himself and what was transpiring. After all, he thought, he wasn't doing anything. Nothing illegal. He was harmless. He wasn't a criminal.

"You're the problem, Peterson. You're stalking my client's kid. And we can't have that. Can we? It's against the law. We tried to warn you. And now you show up here. Not good, Peterson. Not good at all," the ape was speaking low right into Coach's ear, and he could smell his awful breath.

"What a surprise!" Now the second man spoke as he ap-proached the both of them. It surprised Coach. With his back turned to the crowd, he hadn't noticed him walking over to join them.

Coach recognized his voice too.
It was the second man he spoke to on the phone.

"Mr. Peterson shows up at another game," he continued.
The second man was smaller than the first. Darker. Older. Black hair beginning to gray around the edges. Slicked back. Lacquered. Like his partner, he also wore a dark trench coat. He was much classier than the first guy. Handsome. More refined. Definitely the brains of the outfit. He joined the apeman, grabbing on to Coach's other arm, helping to forcefully escort Coach out into the vacating parking lot.

Behind them the crowd began to cheer, clap, hoot and holler. Members of the team were now beginning to emerge from the lower security doors and head up the ramp for the bus.

Coach was unable to turn and look. He had a bodyguard on both sides of him now and they each had a tight grip on his upper arm using it to hastily move him away from the proceedings. If Coach would have been able to look back, he would have seen Edward Travis watching them.

"We saw you in Oakland, Mr. Peterson, but gave you the benefit of the doubt. Seeing how you were in your backyard, so to speak, and you were a basketball coach and all. But then you show up here. More then just a coincidence it seems." Greasy hair was doing all the talking now.

"It's not against the law to go to a game now, is it?" Coach didn't want to seem cocky, but he felt he had to do something. He was becoming too scared to consider acting physically belligerent or defiant. His question was weak and squeaky. The terrifying magnitude of the whole situation was beginning to set in.

"You're right about that Mr. Peterson, but it seems you are taking a special interest in someone we are paid to look out for. I thought we explained that to you over the phone. Thought we made it clear. Thought you understood. Maybe we were wrong."

"Look, maybe I got a little carried away before. But I guarantee you, I'm harmless. Harmless. Western Pacific is a great basketball team. And I love watching them play. You guys know I'm an ex-coach. I just love watching them play." Coach was now pleading. Forget about any braggadocio. Begging would be next.

Peterson! What are you doing, old man? It's not just you! It's Joanie and Michelle too. Have I put them in danger? This is real! Not some . . . it's not Hollywood. Some stupid movie. These guys. . .

"Look, you guys. You're never going to see me again. I swear . . . I promise. I'm harmless. Harmless I tell you. But you're right. This is . . . let me . . . I promise . . . you never see me again. Besides, this is all a mistake. A misunderstanding. It's nothing. Really. Nothing." Coach had started begging.

When they were approximately a hundred yards from the security exit, they began to slow down the pace.

"You love watching them play, but you hang around afterward to see them board the bus." Greasy hair was speaking again. "You're making us all a little nervous, Peterson. What is it exactly that you're up to anyway?"

"Look, I'm telling you. It's nothing. I'm not some kook. You checked me out. I know you have. I'm not bothering anyone," Coach pleaded.

"Put your arms up." It was the ape who grunted. He began to frisk Coach. Coach was compliant.

"This is crazy. I assure you. I'm harmless. What do you think? I'm armed?" Coach said. "This is ridiculous!"

Should I run? Should I yell for help? Yell? They aren't going to do anything here? Are they? Here? In public?

The apeman finished patting him down, and the second man spoke again.

"Look Peterson, we're not going to alert the authorities. We know they won't do jack. We are prepared to act on this entirely independent of the authorities. So don't go thinking you've got rights. That they'll protect you. Innocent until proven guilty. Blah, blah, blah. That isn't how it works, Peterson. We don't give a damn about your rights. So this is it, Peterson. If I ever see you again, if I ever so much as hear your name again, you're going to disappear. For good. Maybe your wife and daughter along with you. You think I'm pulling your leg, Peterson? Don't you? Take my word for it. We're magicians. Poof! You're gone. Poof! Your family is gone. You disappear for good. Now get the hell out of here."

"Yeah, hit the road old man," the ape added. He pushed Coach in the chest hard, and he stumbled away almost losing his balance and going to the pavement.

The two men turned away, both simultaneously brushing their hands off while sneering back at Coach over their shoulders. They walked slowly back toward the crowd and the lights of the bus.

Coach was walking fast now.

He was heading away from the lights of the arena. Not sure of where he was, just as long as it was in a direction away from the bus. Away from Travis. Away from Travis and his henchmen.

Forget the car. Get to the motel. Take a cab. Hike. Climb the fence if you have to. Just go. Move. Move it!

Coach was embarrassed. Ashamed. Humiliated.
And terrified.

How could I be this stupid? What a fool. An old fool. This is real, you idiot. This is real. Go home. Go home! You've go to put an end to this. Go home!
Buy a gun. I'll have to buy a gun! Mess with that. Try to mess with that.
Oh, Joanie. I'm sorry. I'm so sorry. Please forgive me.

He was a considerable distance from the arena now. Almost to the outer fence surrounding the enormous parking lot. It was dark and Coach was hoping he would run into a gate. Some kind of entrance, or exit. But he was prepared to climb a fence if he had to. Whatever it took.

Behind him the sounds had died out. Some headlights. An occasional vehicle. Coach refused to slow down and assess the situation.

He walked past a truck with a camper on it. On the other side of the truck, at first hidden from view, sat a generic compact car. Coach almost walked right past it. He stopped and turned to examine it.

Wait a minute. Is this it? Is this my car? It is! It is! What a break! What a break!

As he was fishing for his keys in his overcoat he realized his shoes were wet. There were puddles throughout the lot and he must have been sloshing right through them as he made his escape. He never noticed. His feet were soaked. He found the keys and unlocked the door. Before getting in he looked over the roof and saw a pair of headlights racing across the lot. They were heading in his direction. The vehicle was moving rapidly, splashing through the puddles as it approached.

Great. Probably security. Just what I need. More questions. If I hurry. . . . Sorry, fellas, I've got to. . . .

It looked like a van of some sort. Coach had opened the door to the rental car and quickly slid into the driver's seat. He looked up at the rearview mirror and watched the vehicle slow down and pull up behind him. The headlights lit up the interior of his vehicle. He put the keys in the ignition and started the car. He heard what sounded like the slam of a sliding door. A van door.

Great. Here they come. Just drive away! Ignore 'em!

Suddenly the driver's side door was yanked open.

What the. . . .

Someone had him by the back of his coat collar and pulled him from the seat, dragging Coach out of the car.

Powerful. . . .

He was struck with a vicious punch. Hard. A fist. Anything else would have killed him. A hard object with that much force behind it would have crushed his skull. The blow landed on the back of Coach's head as he was being dragged from the car. A second strike quickly followed the first one and landed closer to his face. His ear received most of the impact.

A scorching pain shot through his cranium and then was quickly followed by novocaine numbness. It was the kind a prizefighter experiences when receiving the final facial pummeling while trapped in the corner of the ring. As the fighter feels himself being helplessly knocked out, he becomes indifferent to the pain. Pain and fear are disconnected. Before losing sight, sound and balance, he beings to feel only sorrow. Shame and humiliation. Suspended by time and the ropes, the boxer cowers, powerless. His gloved weapons, unwillingly surrendered, hang by his sides. His is rendered an innocent bystander as his past, future and present are destroyed. In a single second before crashing to the canvas, he says a tearful farewell to all his hopes, his dreams, and the confidence he once had of a promising career.

The assailant spun Coach around and punched him in the face. A massive mallet that struck him at once in the mouth and jaw.

There was a loud crack. A gurgle. His wounded face was now covered with blood.

The fear of dying annihilated the pain as Coach was suddenly seized with the horrifying understanding of execution: the terror of the condemned realized. This is really happening. Turns out life's a tragedy, and its ending will be brutal and sadistic.

Murder? I'm being murdered?

He was held by the front of his jacket now. The next violent blow was delivered to his midsection. The air was flushed from his lungs.

Am I going to die? They're going to kill me. This is how it ends? The end. In a parking lot? In Phoenix. . . Fight! Fight! Fight back, Peterson! They're going to. . . .

Too late.

Uppercut.

Coach bent over trying to breathe.

This time the killing fist caught him directly on the nose.

The bones in his face offered little or no resistance.

Coach landed on his back in a large puddle in front of his rental car.

Unconscious.

The puddle slowly began to turn red.

CHAPTER SIXTEEN

MARCH 27, 2004

SATURDAY MORNING 1 A.M.

AMERICA WEST ARENA

PARKING LOT

Ⓘf Coach had laid there any longer he probably would have bled to death.

He was out. Gone. Dropped into a deep and dark abyss. No sight. No sound. Foreign and remote. A domain with no thoughts, images, feelings, dialogue. Dead space. Film broke.

And then at once, in an instant, he was back.

Someone turned the projector back on.

His awaking would always remain some kind of mystery to him. Coach would ponder the scenario for many years to come.

"Now showing. From Omnipotent Productions and Divine Interventions. Brought to you by the Almighty . . . Heavenly Pictures is proud to present. . . ."

Afterwards he used the event as a reminder to himself as to just who was really writing the script.

For some reason being allowed to die in that parking lot was not part of the plot. Not part of his home movie.

When he first opened his eyes he was surprised at how warm and comfortable he felt.

It actually felt quite peaceful, and for a split second he considered staying there. Forever. On his back. In the puddle. Surrender. Sleep. He began to close his eyes.

Final resting place. As good as any. The end.

You did it this time. Boy, you are a classic. Look at you now, nut case. You're in Phoenix. Lying in a puddle with the crap kicked out of you. "Hey Warriors! Check out your beloved and esteemed coach. Say good-bye. It's the last time you'll see him. If he does live you'll find him in the cuckoo's nest. Locked up."

Despite the seemingly desperate situation, to Coach there was something humorous about the whole thing. Absurd as it was, he felt a little amused. After all, this was going to bring closure to the madness, and that realization made Coach feel a great sense of relief. Content. For a moment he felt happy. He even feigned a smile.

Then he tried to sit up.

And the pain came.

Lay down! Lay back down! You blew it, buddy. See where all your lies got you? Should have quit when you were ahead. Thought you knew all about that. Quitting when you were ahead. Whoops! Wife was right again! Bless her heart. Forget it. Sayonara. Adios, amigo.

Shock! How long have I been laying here? This is real, you fool! You're dying! Shock can kill you! Remember the training? The classes? First Aid? CPR? You're dying! This is the real thing!

At the same time, Coach realized there was something unusual about the puddle he was laying in. It wasn't just rainwater. The puddle he sat in was mostly blood! The realization jolted him. Inspiration ignition! Although the warranty had run out a long time ago, and it could be already be classified as an antique, the agitation managed to jump start his adrenaline engine.

Is that blood? That can't be blood. Oh my God! Oh my God! Get up! Get up!

He lifted his hands to his face and discovered his nose was still bleeding. He was choking on the blood in his throat. He had no way of knowing his ears were bleeding too.

I can't breathe! I can hardly breath! You're going to die, you idiot! Get up! Get up!

He wouldn't find out until later his ribs were cracked.

The car! Get in the car! It's running? The car is still running? The headlights are on. Door's open. That's good. That's good. Have to get in the car!

Maybe if it was just him he would have chosen the puddle.
Given up. Acquiesced to the pain and the shame.
But he knew it wasn't just about him.
It was Joanie.
And Michelle.
He loved them. Loved them very much. And even though they sometimes drove him crazy, he wasn't ready to give them up.
Leave them? He thought. Not an option.
Abruptly. Desperately. He realized he needed to see them. To tell them he loved them. To tell them the truth. Make things right. Beg them for forgiveness.

Live.
Live.

To survive and take care of Joanie. She deserved better. She had given him so much. Stayed with him. Believed in him. Believed in him when he even doubted himself.

Maybe there was more to life. Maybe it could be more. So what? He was a Peterson! And Petersons didn't quit. Petersons didn't give up. And Petersons didn't leave.

I'm selfish. I'm a selfish old fool. What could be worse? Get up! Get up and go home!

He used his arms to help get his feet under him.

I can't do it.
The pain. Oh man.
Isn't there anyone around? Help. Help me. This is serious! I'm a mess. Peterson, it's worse than you think. Much worse!

He was gasping for air. The cracked ribs along with his smashed nose made it very difficult to draw a breath. He couldn't speak. Couldn't yell for help. Blood everywhere. And his soaked overcoat seemed to weigh a thousand pounds.

I'm covered in blood! I can't do this! I'm going to die? No way! No way!

He stumbled into the front of the car, using the bumper and hood to help pull himself to his feet.

I can't see! Go! Go! Get in! Blow the horn! Maybe someone will come. Maybe someone will hear. I can do this! I can do this! Oh man, you need some help. Someone. . . .

He used the car to hold himself up, and he slid around the hood to the driver's side. He left trails of blood wherever his hands touched the surface of the car.

Did they leave me here to die? They left me here to die. Look at this! This is. . . .

He was halfway in the car now.

The legs. Get the legs in.

He had to use his hands and arms to help lift and drag his legs into the car. His arms and legs helped him to maneuver his legs into position under the steering wheel.

Now the horn. Blow the horn!

The wipers came on.

Where's the horn?

He couldn't find it.

Drive! Drive! Just drive!

He reached over and shifted the car. It took off careening across the lot toward the boulevard. No horn. No vision. Only the wipers. His legs had very little feeling in them and he had the gas pedal pressed to the floor. The car smashed through a chain link fence. For a moment it felt like the fence was going to hold the car back, but it finally tore through, and Coach went careening down the street. Blurred vision. Like he was under-water at night in a pool with lights going thirty-five miles an hour.

Can't see! A gas station. Is that a gas station? I can't tell. Got to slow down. I can't feel my legs. My feet. The brakes! Hit the brakes!

Maybe it was because he had competed all his life.

Life was one big game.
One big competition to Coach.
Not just the basketball.
It was the day-to-day stuff.
Stay sober.
Keep your job.
Prove yourself.
Stay fit.
Eat responsibly.
Keep your wife. Stay married.
Face life without your son.
Live with the guilt.
Keep the faith.

It was all one big competition. One long and arduous campaign. It had to be. Coach had to make it that way or he would have given up a long time ago.

Keep going.
Get back up.

He loved players that hated to lose. He loved players that refused to accept defeat. That is where the thrill of competition lies. The joy. The exhilaration. It was found in the effort. It had to be supreme. It had to be all out. Everything you had. Therein lies the satisfaction. Exhausted on the field. Knowing you gave it everything.

Competition.

Competition is never giving up. Only when you give up do you suffer defeat.

Challenge yourself. Challenge yourself. Everyday. How else could I have made it through each and every day these past few years? How else?

Most of the criticism of Coach during his career came from his obsession with winning.

But Coach believed that any player worth anything deep down inside loved the hard work and appreciated the discipline. To Coach, it wasn't the winning, but the trying to win that meant everything. And he wanted his players to believe in the same thing. Success could only be found when a person did everything they could to try and win. Trying to win. That was the on ramp for the road to success. It didn't matter if it led anywhere. It was the trip that counted. The journey that counted.

The virtues? They were simple. Devotion to God, family, the game and his charges. Coach believed that the oldest virtues stood the test of time. They endured through the changes in our society. They were things like honesty, hard work, integrity, responsibility, loyalty.

And humility.

When the success came, the hardware, the acclaim, that was the most difficult to handle. Coach didn't wear his religion on his sleeve, but it definitely affected what he tried to teach. Great athletes, as well as great coaches, were given a gift. And it was important to worship the giver of that gift, and not the gift itself. When you used that talent, when you used that gift to your fullest capability, you glorified God.

He jumped the curb and was almost able to hit the breaks in time before crashing into a pick-up truck parked next to the gas pumps.

That hurt. The seat belt! You forgot the seat belt, stupid!

He opened the door and fell out onto the cement.

I'm not going to die! Not tonight! No way.

He heard voices.
They were cussing at him. "Crazy mudda. . . ."

Are they cussing at me? "Hey, watch your language! I'll make you run sprints for that!"

He saw faces. Angry, disgusted faces, looking down at him.

Sorry about the truck.

He passed out.

CHAPTER SEVENTEEN

MARCH 28, 2004

SUNDAY

ST. JOHN'S HOSPITAL

PHOENIX, ARIZONA

Most of Saturday was still a little vague.

Besides having a concussion, he was heavily sedated. The ability to think clearly came and went. But each time he awoke, he remembered a little more.

He knew that he was in the critical care unit of a local Phoenix hospital. He had a fractured jaw, broken nose, and two cracked ribs. It was difficult to talk and difficult to move.

His recollection of how he got there only came in pieces. He remembered waking up for a short time in the ambulance. He was panicking when he awoke, yet the paramedics were acting very casual about his condition.

Help me! I'm not just some wino off the street!

He remembered lying in a semiconscious state in the emergency room for what seemed like forever.

Two female doctors, Doctor Altman and a Doctor Ailbee, however, acted swiftly and professionally. Coach always read the name tags. Even in the grocery store. He remembered the

151

doctors reassuring him his injuries were not as bad as they appeared. The loss of blood was a concern but not as severe as he might have thought. It was the mixture of blood and the rainwater that made it appear that way.

When they were finished cleaning him up and he was wheeled from the emergency ward, he felt confident that he was going to live.

He fell asleep.

On Sunday afternoon when he awoke, a nurse was at work in his room.

"Well, look who is awake," she said.

She was a middle-aged woman, heavy set, dark hair with some streaks a gray beginning to sneak in. She had a round friendly face, and a warm friendly smile.

"Mr. Peterson comes back to join the living. I'll bet you're hungry?" she continued.

"You know my name?" asked Coach.

"Of course we do. We lifted your wallet. Had to look for an insurance card or we would have thrown you out on your good ear," she laughed at her own jokes.

Coach liked her immediately.

"I've got to call my wife," Coach announced.

"Oh shucks! Another married one. Cripes sake! Wouldn't you know it. I never get lucky in this job."

She moved very quickly around the room doing her job, all the time chatting and laughing.

"Well, you know what? Now that you're awake I'll call down to special services and they'll get someone up here to help you out with all that stuff. First the doctor needs to see you. Then the PD. Seems they want to know where that banana peel is you slipped on last night."

"Hey, you should see the other guy," it was difficult for Coach to joke around with his fractured jaw.

"OK, Mike Tyson," the nurse was laughing again. "Meanwhile, do you want some help seeing a man about a horse?"

"No, I think I'm fine for now," Coach said, but was deciding he was in too much pain to try and continue trading barbs with the nurse.

"All right then, let me go make my calls, and I'll see if I can find you something that's edible. How about a T-bone steak and some lobster? Surf and turf. I'll see if our chef can puree it for you. We got to get you healthy so you can resume your career in the rodeo. Meanwhile, if you need anything, give me a buzz. Margaret is on the job. A nursey with mercy."

"Thanks, Margaret," Coach managed.

"Oh, don't mention it. Someday they're going to actually pay me for this job."

With that she was out the door, still laughing in the hallway.

Coach felt a great sense of relief.

I'm going to live. I could still make my flight tomorrow. Maybe I don't need to call Joanie. I could tell her everything when I get home. Tell her everything. Come clean. What a relief that will be. But the police. What am I going to tell them? More lies?

When two Phoenix detectives finally showed up Coach just stuck to the bare facts.

He didn't embellish any of the details, and use any kind of conjecture. He merely answered the questions that were asked. He hadn't seen the face of the man who hit him. Didn't get a license plate.

He could tell right away by their questions in the scheme of things the incident wasn't going to get too much attention by the Phoenix Police Department. It was an assault. Big deal.

Unfortunately they had to deal with thousands of those a year. It was a testament to the violence they had to constantly deal with on a daily basis.

"OK. The guy got jumped. For some reason they didn't take his wallet."

"They broke his nose. His jaw."

"He lived."

"Move on."

"Next."

If the two detectives that questioned him had any suspicions, they played indifferent. Didn't seem to care.

Luckily, they hadn't bothered to ask the right questions, and their overall lack of concern was OK with Coach. He was greatly relieved when they started to put away their notepads and finally left. All Coach wanted to do was get home as quickly as possible. The damage to his psyche was worse than the damage to his face. He had to try not to make anyone too suspicious and turn this into a Grand Jury investigation.

He just wanted to get on the plane and leave as quickly as possible.

After all, what was I supposed to do? Accuse Edward Travis? That would be suicide. Those two detectives would have had me locked up. A lunatic. "So what were you exactly doing in Phoenix? Following Edward Travis around, huh?" Edward Travis could make me look like the guilty one. He could make himself look like the victim. And you? You would look like an idiot if this got in the papers and reached back home. "Well folks, it's time to change the name on the old gym. Turns out the old Coach is a loony. A stalker." Edward Travis was willing to kill me to get me to back off, to kill me for showing up at a lousy basketball game. For looking him up on the internet. Wake up, Peterson! This is the real world!

Coach fell into another deep sleep after the detectives left, after struggling with a bowl of chicken broth Nurse Margaret brought him.

When he finally awoke he thought it might be in the middle of the night, one, two, maybe three in the morning, but it was only eight P.M.

He was startled by a man sitting next to his bed.

He was dressed in a suit, sitting in a chair, reading the *Phoenix Sun Times* sports section.

Coach's stomach did a somersault.

Oh boy, here goes!

"Mr. Peterson! Mr. Peterson. You're awake. How you feeling? Like crap, huh? You must, cuz you look like crap. No offense, you know. It could have been a lot worse. And the doctor says you're going to be just fine. Probably be released tomorrow." When the stranger stopped talking he sat there smiling down at Coach.

Friend or Foe? Something different. Does he know me?

"Who are you?" asked Coach.
"My name is Brian. Brian's the name, investigation's the game."

Great. Another detective.

"What do you want? I already told you guys everything I know," said Coach.
"I know that," said Brian. "Saw the police report myself."
"So, what is it you want?" Coach inquired.
"Just a couple more things I was hoping you could help me out with?" Brian asked.
Detective Brian was young. Coach recognized the fact that there was something distinctly different about Brian. Different from the first two detectives that interrogated him. He wasn't exactly sure how. Couldn't put his finger on it. Just different.

Better dressed, that's for sure. Looks like his suit didn't come off a rack. Good looking. Sharp. A lot sharper. Sharper looking. Sharper dressed. Accent? His accent is different. Something. Much more sophisticated than the other two guys.

"A couple more things, eh? And they would be?" Coach asked.

"Well, Mr. Peterson, I can't help wondering. It was awfully late last night when you were assaulted. There wasn't anyone around. No witnesses. How come it took you so long to leave? To leave the game?"

"I told the police this afternoon. I got lost leaving the arena," said Coach trying to sound exasperated, and was now staring up at the ceiling.

"OK. So what did you do while the place was emptying? Did you wander around the whole time looking for your car?" Brian asked.

"Yeah, mostly," Coach answered. He was again reminded of how difficult it was to speak with his injured jaw.

"Well, Coach, you were there so long. You probably saw the teams leaving. Getting on the bus. You couldn't have missed that did you?" inquired Brian.

"I saw a bus. I didn't see the players get on it. Or the bus leave," Coach responded.

"Did you see the people standing around waiting for the players?" Brian continued.

"Yeah, some of them," answered Coach.

"See anybody you knew?" Brian asked.

Coach knew he was in trouble now. How was he going to answer this one without lying?

No more lies. No mas! Put an end to the lies. The lying.

"Yeah. I did," Coach answered with a little hesitation.

"Oh yeah. Who did you see?" Brian queried.

"I saw Edward Travis," Coach admitted.

"Oh yeah! The famous movie producer. Standing out there in the lot with the rest of the fans. Imagine that! That takes guts for someone so famous. Probably was surrounded by body-guards though. Protection. Keep the autograph hounds away. The guy has some bucks. Mega rich. The guy has made a mint from those R-rated slash movies he produces. Huh?"

"Yeah, I guess. Who are you anyway?" Coach suddenly blurted out. He was starting to get a little nervous. Angry. This wasn't your typical police interrogation.

"Answer me this, Mr. Peterson. Did Edward Travis see you? Do you think he saw you?"

"How would I know? He might have." Coach was now getting even more anxious.

No lies! No more lies!

He thought about buzzing the nurse, or the doctor. "Hey, who are you? Could I see some identification?"

"I'm someone who is trying to help you, Mr. Peterson. A friend. I'll tell you what. I'll let you get some more sleep. You need to take care of yourself. There are some people out there who need you, Coach. Care about you. Care about you a great deal."

He got up to go. Before he reached the door he stopped, then he turned around to look back at Coach. He was smiling again.

"Oh by the way. I thought you might be interested. Western Pacific won today. They're heading for the Final Four. That Travis kid is something else. He's a talented son of a gun. Don't know where he gets it. His old man sure looks like a wimp to me. A real dweeb. Well, Mr. Peterson, I gotta go." He continued to smile down at Coach for a few more seconds before continuing. "You take care of yourself now. I'll be in touch."

Who was that guy? And whose side is he on? I thought he might even be a Travis guy coming back to finish the job. Did he call me Coach once?

Well, I'm leaving tomorrow. No matter what. They're not gonna keep me here. I'm going home. I swear. I'm never leaving home again.

Forgive me.

Please forgive me.

Oh Lord, you've bailed me out so many times. Help me here.
For Joanie.
I've got to see her again. Make things right.
For Joanie.
For Michelle.

A short time later Coach was fast asleep again.

The nurse woke Coach up in the middle of the night.
Medication time. It was a different nurse. He didn't recognize her. He was too groggy to make small talk. She didn't seem too interested in it anyway. There was just enough light from the hallway to see the clock on the night stand. It was two o'clock in the morning.
The hospital was quiet. Dark.
Everyone once in a while he could here the muffled sounds of the nurses whispering outside the rooms. He awoke with some more pain. Pain in new places. His neck and back now ached along with his face and ribs.

Figures. You're always sorer the next day. "Well, join the party. All aches and pains invited." I still don't care. If I can't walk, I'll crawl out of here. Hospitals. To think my mother and my sister Doreen spent their whole life working in one of these places. All the pain. The misery. Makes teaching a dream job. I'd take a back-talking teenager any day.

Coach started to think about his last visitor. Last night. Brian.

Probably a Travis guy. He's out there right now coming down the hall pushing a scrub bucket. Dressed as a custodian. A pistol with a silencer attached. "Gotta finish off the old man. Shut him up." I've seen too many movies. Seen too many of Travis type movies.
I'm leaving today. Leaving.

Coach had an early afternoon flight.

What about the rental car? Wonder what happened to it. Should have paid extra for that insurance. Would have got my money out of that one.

It was too painful to laugh but a chuckle escaped anyway. Just the thought of being hours away from returning to California made him feel a little better.

The motel. Have to swing by and pick up my things. Never even unpacked. Never even slept in the bed. Never bought that six pack.
"Load me up with meds, Nurse Margaret. I'm hitting the road. Gonna sleep in my own bed tonight. And every night hereafter. Can't stay here. Nope. The hospital life ain't for me."
Wow, it must be the drugs. I'm starting to feel better. Stoned again! In just a few hours. I can do this. "So long, Phoenix. So long, hospital."
You know the last time I was in a hospital was for Parker's birth? Up all night helping Joanie.
What a miracle.
An absolute miracle.
Happiest day of my life.
Everybody says that. But for me, there is no doubt. Happiest day of my life. Makes you wonder, don't it, how can anyone abandon a child? How could anyone even consider that? Parker. Giddiness was now replaced with sorrow, and tears swelled up in Coach's eyes.
To leave a child.
How could anyone do that?

Western Pacific won!

Coach reached for the TV remote.

SportsCenter. Perfect timing.

They were just beginning to show the highlights of the Western Pacific-Oklahoma game.

The game wasn't as close as everyone expected.

Oklahoma couldn't zone press the Pirates. The Pirates were able to get their jailbreak offense into high gear. Use their speed.

The Sooner attempt to press cost them tons of early fast-break baskets by Western Pacific.

Western Pacific, on the other hand, hurt the Sooners with its full court pressure. When the Sooners were able to set up their half court zone, the Pirates bombed away. Skip passes resulted in wide open looks and three-point bombs. Lester Travis had 3 of them in the first half. Once during the highlights, after showing a Travis three, they flashed to Edward Travis sitting in the stands, showing his approval.

The Pirates led by 11 at the half.

The tough match-up everyone expected never materialized. Early in the second half Oklahoma did make a brief run. They got within 5. But Western Pacific quickly answered with a 10 point run putting the game in a comfort zone the rest of the way.

With five minutes to go Oklahoma had to go man to man. Something that wasn't part of their game. Something no one had forced them to do all year. It was ugly, and Western Pacific chewed it up. They won by 27.

Lester Travis finished with 25 points, 12 assists, 10 rebounds. A triple double.

He was named the MVP.

Western Pacific was going to the Final Four in San Antonio.

The next morning, Coach Peterson went home.

CHAPTER EIGHTEEN

APRIL 2, 2004

FRIDAY

AT HOME IN THE BACKYARD

Presidents' Day.

That holiday in February signaled it was time for the annual trimming of the backyard rose bushes. Most years Coach's teams were busy. Traveling deep into the playoffs. Most years the bushes had to wait until March to get their trimming.

Actually, in all the years he was coaching the roses were only trimmed in February once. It was probably more about procrastination than anything else. He liked to wait for that first warm and sunny weekend that begged him to be outside and help welcome the arrival of spring.

Presidents' Day did, however, serve as a reminder that it was time for Coach to start thinking about getting his clippers out. Getting them sharpened. Push his rusty wheel barrow out back to his seventeen rose bushes (there used to be twenty-one but over the years he had casualties), and start cutting them back. He also had to make sure the fences were strong so the deer wouldn't feast on his blossoms (which seemed to happen at least once during the summer no matter how cautious he was).

Joanie definitely had the green thumb in the family. But she wasn't as big a rose fan as Coach. So she left their care up to him. Coach loved them.

Maybe it was because no matter how bad he butchered them, they always seemed to bloom throughout the summer anyway. Over the course of the summer he took special care trimming and cutting the blossoms which he carefully and periodically put in a vase on the dining room table. He was very proud of his roses. And over the years they became his exclusive yard responsibility, along with cutting the grass and pulling the weeds.

The Friday after Coach got back from Phoenix was the first actual warm day Empire had seen in a while. The rains had lingered in the foothills a bit longer this year. But today the weatherman had said it would remain partly sunny and the temperature might climb into the high sixties.

Coach was up early.

Psyching himself up for the annual assault. It was always the first yard job he chose to do when spring arrived. Always placed ahead of the nasty job of raking and burning the pine needles.

The sun hadn't yet climbed through the trees, but it was warming up quickly, and he had already hung his jacket on the back porch railing.

The streaks of sunlight that leaked through the ponderosas felt warm and soothing on Coach's sore face. Every once in a while he would look up from his work and turn toward the sunshine. Facing the sun with his eyes closed, he would wait while his face was tranquilized by the rays of the sun.

He would remain in that position for a few minutes gazing up at the sun feeling like it possessed some special healing powers. Special powers that could not only take away his soreness, but could relieve the pain that was located deeper down inside.

Down near the roots.

He was hoping the sun had the power to turn back the clock to a time when his muscles were young and green, and used to welcome a test or an opportunity to show how healthy and strong they had become.

Maybe the sun that restores life and renews the blossoms to his bushes could somehow nurture his own well being.

Remove the droop in his back. Eliminate the stiffness in his neck.

Allow him to stand straight and strong again.

And renew his ability, and his will, to grow again.

When Parker disappeared, so many parts of Coach began to disappear along with him. Parts began to die off. Dreams and desires. His volition and determination. All sick. Withering. Rotting with decay.

Piece by piece.

Little by little.

Dying.

Dying on the vine.

Coach was only alive when it was tied with two minutes to go.

That is all that was left.

The thrill of the hunt.

The thrill of the kill.

Brief. Short-lived signs of life. And then dormancy again.

He stood now with the rose bush clippers in his hand staring up at the sun, and he realized how selfish and greedy he had become.

It was true.

Joanie was right.

He was obsessed with coaching before Parker. It was even worse after he was gone.

It was the only thing he kept alive after they lost him. The only part of his life he nurtured.

Addicted.

He was addicted. The same way he was addicted to alcohol. A disease.

Winning. His only goal.

Had to have it.

Couldn't live without it.

Too many other things in his life had been set aside. He didn't know when he crossed the line, but it was progressive, just like the alcohol. It got worse as the years went by. Out of control. Much worse, after Parker. The need. The desire. And it became more and more impossible to subdue.

The planning.

The pursuit.

The adrenaline rush.

Sleepless nights before a game.

The caffeine poisoning during the play-offs.

Eat on the run. Sleep on the run. Take care of your family on the run.

Focus. Focus. No distractions.

Win. Win. One more. One more time. That's all that mattered.

His life could only be justified by twenty win seasons.

In the end I thought it would mean something. Was that the reason why I lost Parker? Selfishness. Winning. The game. Always the game. I always said family, then religion before anything else. Was that really true?

Joanie used to accuse Coach of going into a post season depression every year.

She said that it didn't matter how successful the season was, he grew silent and moped around. Nobody or nothing deserved his attention. She had to continue to do all the domestics long after the balls were put away.

Pay the bills. Go to the store. Call the plumber. Get the car fixed. All Joanie.

Where was I? Joanie needed me. She needed me. I let her die too.

It didn't matter now that he had more time than ever. Nothing changed. He had remained in that state of mind since he retired. It was just more of the same. Coach, and coaching first. Everything else tied for second.

Joanie. Joanie. She had to do everything. Still does. What have you done? What have you given her lately? These last few years? Few years? Try twenty. Try twenty years. Nothing. Nothing. That's what you've given her. Absolutely nothing.

And now that he didn't have a season to look forward to. To recharge his batteries. To get his fix. There were even fewer signs of life.

Unkempt. Unpruned. Dying.

Of course he denied it.
Denial.

I'm good at denial. Great at denial. A virtual superstar.

Standing in his garden that morning he knew now that it was all true.

I hated it when the season came to an end. Even as exhausted as I was when it was over, I hated it. Hated it to end. And when it came time to put the balls away for good . . . it was even worse.

I have not appreciated Joanie enough. Haven't loved her. Cherished her. She made my life all work, and in my obsessive and selfish way I took her for granted. All my life I preached about teamwork. "Teamwork's the key. Can't win without the teamwork. There is no 'I' in team." Turns out, I was the most selfish player of all. Everything had to be about me. I'm the reason I lost Parker. I'm the reason I lost Joanie. We had a covenant and I broke it.

Anger.

Everybody thinks their life should be perfect. Everybody thinks that they deserve it. But the truth. . . . The truth is . . . life is a bittersweet miracle. A bittersweet miracle. At best. Magic and tragic. That's all. Magic and tragic.

Depression.

I hated to lose. Losing anything. I just couldn't handle it. And that included my basketball seasons . My coaching career. My job. My son. Winning was a blessing. But it had its downside too. To whom much is given . . . much will be asked in return. I took, but what did I give back?

Acceptance.

Acceptance. I just can't get there. Sometimes I think I am. But I'm not. No way. Just can't get there.

Coach was on his last bush.
Joanie was up. He could hear her talking and laughing.

Was she on the phone? Must be on the phone. She wasn't even out of bed yet when I came out here to work. It was like . . . 7 when I got out here. Can't be 9 yet. Did I hear the doorbell? Someone at the door? This early?

A flash of paranoia.
Fear.
He straightened up from his work and began to head for the steps of the back deck to investigate. Before he climbed the gradual slope leading to the stairs, the sliding door was pulled open. Sara Rick stepped through and out onto the deck. She was looking back over her shoulder and saying something to Joanie about having to "talk to the old codger herself."
Coach's apprehension subsided. He didn't have to worry. Not about Sara. He had told Joanie everything.

True confessions. Thank goodness. Don't have to worry about Sara. Might have to tell Sara the rest of the story though. As embarrassing as it is. Should tell her.

Coach had learned one thing about life from coaching. Tragedy can turn to comedy in a short period of time.

He had this player. She was a post. But she always wanted to be a guard even though she was six foot two and burley. She was a tough physical inside player and the only rebounder on the team. However, she always was looking to score from the outside. Shoot the three. She would wander out to the perimeter trying to get open just like the wings or guards. Coach had the hardest time trying to convince her of what her role was.

A rebounder. A post defender. A screener.

She was on a team filled with very prolific scorers, and she had an uncontrollable desire to be one of them. The other thing was she was always attempting these fancy passes. At times when a very simple chest pass or bounce pass would get the job done, she would attempt a circus pass, throw a no look, or a behind the back pass.

One night in the championship game of a pre-season tournament, the Warriors were tied with thirty seconds left. She pulled down a tough defensive rebound, but instead of out-letting it to a guard, she took off down the middle of the court dribbling precariously through the retreating defensive traffic. When she got to the free-throw line of her offensive end of the court, she came to jump stop and threw this no look behind the back pass to the person on her right who was streaking toward the basket.

It was the referee.

The referee ducked and the pass landed in the third row. The other team got the ball out of bounds, ran the clock down, and scored at the buzzer to win.

Coach, of course, was furious. It took everything to control his anger while the other team celebrated. He was still beside himself during the awards ceremony. Couldn't even so much as look in the direction of the post player who turned the ball over. He was afraid he might explode.

The loss hung on him for days.

By the following year Coach would tell the story many times. It would always illicit a great deal of laughter. His assistant coach, Willie Dutra, loved to tell the story too. Maybe sitting at the bar at a coaching clinic. He loved to tell it even more when Coach was present. Everyone roared, because they all knew how much Coach hated to lose. It became one of their favorite stories.

Tragedy turns to comedy.

Coach hoped that someday they could all laugh about him getting beat up in Phoenix.

"Hey Coach," Sara said as she came down the steps of the deck.

"Sara. Good morning. What in God's earth are you doing here? And so early in the morning? I mean it's good to see you and all, but what a surprise." Coach was smiling. It was still always good to see Sara.

"Well, I flew into Reno late last night." Sara seemed to be almost trying to catch her breath.

As she came down the steps toward where Coach was standing, he thought she looked a little ragged around the edges. Sleepless maybe.

Is that concern on her face? She looks worried? Sara's never worried. Now what?

"What did you do? Stay up all night gambling? You need a loan to get home?" Coach joked.

"Didn't lose a penny. Too late. Too tired. Heard you got the shit beat out of you in Phoenix, Coach," she teased. Laughing. Same ol' Sara. It brought Coach some relief.

"Sara, watch your language! Well, you didn't come all this way just to give me a hard time about that, did you? Who told you anyway? Joanie tell you?" Coach was still a little unsettled. A little anxious. Suspicious.

Now what? What now? Sara looks worried. She's worried. She never looks this serious. She's clutch. Doesn't get rattled. Never rattled.

"Coach," she said very quietly while lowering her head as she continued to slowly move toward where he stood amongst his roses.

"Coach," she started a second time. She was standing in front of him now. Three feet. Looking up at him.

Is she crying? Sure is breathing heavy. Out of shape? Smoking again, I'll bet.

"What's wrong, Sara? What is it?" Coach said as he reached out to take Sara's hand. "What is it? Tell me."

"Coach," Sara now said for a third time.

She is. She's crying. I've never seen Sara cry. Never. I can't remember. . . .

"Coach. He's your son. He's your son. Lester Travis *is* Parker, Coach. He's your son." Sara began to cry. "It all checked out. The DNA samples. Fingerprints. All of it. You were right, Coach. Lester Travis is Parker."

Tears began to roll down her cheeks.

"Oh Sara. Sara." He was rocking back and forth on his feet. "Sara," Coach repeated. His knees got weak. Dizzy. Vertigo.

At first it didn't sink in. How could it sink in?

What did she say? Did I hear her correctly. She said . . . she said . . .

The tears came for him too. He reached for her. They held each other. Held each other up with their embrace.

"It's true, Coach. It's true. You were right, Coach. I can't believe it myself. Crazy. Crazy. It's true, Coach. You were right."

Am I going to pass out? Faint. I can't stand up! Is this what fainting feels like? My knees! My legs! They're not working. I'm falling! I'm. . . . It can't be. . . .

Sara took her head off Coach's shoulder and put her hand on the side of his face.

"Your kid's a pretty good player, Coach." She held him again. Hugged him. He was sobbing.

He was afraid to let go. Afraid he would fall over.

"Joanie," he looked up at the decks sliding door. He could barely get her name out. "Joanie," a little louder now. "Joanie," now as loud as Coach's battered face would allow. He began to let go of Sara. Turned back toward her. "Did you tell Joanie? Did you tell her yet?"

"What? What is it?" Joanie said as she was throwing open the sliding screen door.

Now looking down at the two of them she stopped and much quieter said it again.

"What is it?" Joanie asked.

"No, I haven't, Coach. I thought you should be the one," Sara said as Coach headed for the steps to the deck.

"Parker. Parker's alive, Joanie! Parker's alive! It was him. It is him. He's Lester. Lester Travis," Coach said as he half stumbled up the steps.

Joanie stood still for a moment and closed her eyes. She was holding two cups of coffee in her hands. She started to shake and the coffee began to spill over the sides. Coach got to Joanie before she dropped the mugs. Before she fell. Collapsed.

He helped ease her down on a patio chair, took the coffee from her hands and set them on the patio table. Joanie bent over holding her face in her two trembling hands. Coach knelt down beside her and put his head in her lap. She took her hands, wet from trying to hold back her own tears, and placed them on Coach's cheeks, holding his swollen face between them.

It had been a long time since they held each other. Touched.

Long enough that neither one could remember. Silent and distant days filled up the last sixteen years, and the years they spent in love had become distant an empty memories.

They had been doomed for over sixteen years. Given a crippling virus that forced them to live independently of each other. Rogues in their own little kingdom.

Forced to exist in some surreal state where they only caught glimpses of each other. Existing in parallel universes. When they reached out to touch each other, they were left holding nothing. Nothing but more loneliness and despair. How they both had longed to be together again. To turn back the clock. To hold one another's hand once again.

Speak softly.

Kiss.

They so desperately needed each other. Ached for atonement. But the curse would not have any of that. Sadness. Misery. Grief. That was all that was allowed. They were permitted to see each other, but had to remain separated by some three-dimensional wall, unable to break through to the other side.

As they held each other now and silently wept in each others arms, they both knew it was over. Over.

The curse had been lifted.

They could be together again.

They could be a family again.

"I hope you guys aren't planning on staying like that all morning?" It was Sara who spoke and broke the silence.

Sara Rick was having a tough time trying to keep her composure too.

"You know you guys can't stay like that all day. We've got to get going. We've got a game to see."

CHAPTER NINETEEN

APRIL 3, 2004

SATURDAY

ALAMODOME DOME

SAN ANTONIO

The college game was now primarily dominated by young brash coaches.

Many of them were ex-players of some of the greatest coaches to have ever been involved in the game.

The Wizard. The General. The Dean. They were all ancient history now.

When they began to disappear, so did the styles of play they had originated. Unfortunately, so did much of their philosophies. Philosophies of discipline and team play. It was a players' game now. There were five "I's" in team. The younger coaches were now the most successful recruiters offering the players the most freedom. Unfortunately, many times they offered improper inducements along with it. It didn't seem to bother many of the new coaches that many players openly admitted they only planned to stay around a year or two before they made themselves available for the NBA draft.

It was obvious that the new breed didn't care as much about building character or trying to make someone a better person, or construct a better player for that matter. Their focus was to win. Bottom line. Win. Win now. Period. Disregard chemistry and use the "quick fix" method if you have to.

The days of a coach who stuck to a system of team discipline were over.

There were no dictators allowed. The demands of individual play managed to finally drive most of the old guys out. Players were now raised to feel empowered and played with a sense of entitlement. Played like it was their right to be on the team. Certainly not a privilege. Most of the young players were so self-centered, they felt like it was a privilege for the coach to have him or her on their team. The coach should be the one who's grateful.

That sense of empowerment which started in the Pros had filtered down to the colleges. And now it was beginning to permeate the high school game too, inflaming teenage self-importance more than ever before. Most talented players were spoiled, undisciplined and lacked fundamentals.

They were basically uncoachable. And the lessons in life, the honorable value system that could be imbued through their relationship with strong leadership, those things were no longer part of the equation. Players wanted instant gratification and there were a lot of coaches around willing to give it to them. They were inclined to sacrifice their own integrity trying to find a short cut to the top.

But, like Coach Peterson always said, "Teams that got to the top of the mountain weren't dropped there."

The way Coach Peterson saw it, most coaches today were far from role models and mentors. They were lightweights. Glorified baby-sitters. Or they were politicians kissing babies, and telling everyone just what they wanted to hear.

Because today's athletes needed so much pampering and required so much unwarranted flattery, most coaches didn't stay around long. The demands were too great. Too costly. They became frustrated, burned out, fired or run off by a trenchant faultfinding media or backbiting acrimonious parents suffering from *parentis vociferous*. Or, they became victims of overzealous alumni with selfish expectations. And when the pressure was brought to bear by these various factions, most of the coaches lacked any kind of principles to fall back on.

Either the coach moved on, or the players did. Transfers were popping up everywhere. Players and coaches were becoming mercenaries. Loud, intrusive parents, who thought of the game as extensions of their own lives, were shopping their kids around like street pimp daddies looking for a payday and a big package of promises.

The irony, of course, was that no team filled with McDonald's All Americans ever won everything. There were a lot of impostors, teams filled with super individuals, but ultimately the team that played selflessly and made the sacrifices wound up wearing the crown.

Winning the ring was important to most kids these days, but having the stats to get your name in the paper was primary.

Exposure was much more important than experience.

Western Pacific's next opponent, Kentucky, was such a team. Kentucky was a multi-talented team in the middle of an NCAA investigation.

All of a sudden there was a lot more at stake in the tournament. Coach's *son* was playing in it. Parker was playing. He was playing in the Final Four. His son, who was one of the best players in the country, had a chance to win the National Championship.

Things began to happen very fast.

There was little regard for sleep. Coach barely remembers packing. But the three of them, Joanie, Sara, and Coach, had boarded a red-eye out of Sacramento for San Antonio on Friday night. There was a short debate about calling Michelle. Joanie was apprehensive. She wanted to wait. Coach agreed only

because he sensed how fragile she was. She was still a nonbe-
liever.

Sara had been on the phone the last twenty-four hours. She
didn't even get a chance to take a break on the plane. She went
back and forth between her associates and listening into conference calls with the attorneys of Edward Travis. Every once in a
while she took a minute to tell Joanie and Coach what was
transpiring. There were so many legal issues she explained. It
was complicated. Very complicated.

But it was very simple to Coach.

He wanted to see his son.

And he was not about to let all the mumbo jumbo, legal this
and legal that, get in his way.

Right now, according to Coach, one of the prime consider-
ations had to be Lester Travis' well being as a basketball player.

That should be a chief concern. He was playing in the most
important game of his life, and that needed to be taken into
consideration. That was the one thing that made the situation
complicated for Coach. He was a little edgy about that issue,
and a little dismayed that nobody else was concerned about it as
much as he was.

Same ol' Coach!

The federal team of lawyers was headed by Brian Anderberg. It turns out he was the investigative lawyer who questioned Coach in the hospital, and he had very little regard for
the fact that a basketball game had to be played. He was out to
nail Edward Travis. And the tournament didn't really concern
him. It wasn't even in the top one hundred.

They were proceeding as cautiously as they could. To them,
there was a much bigger picture here. It had to do with kidnapping, possible illegal adoption schemes, and the forgery of state
and federal documents. To them it was Edward Travis, but it
was a whole lot more. It was much deeper. They knew that with

Edward Travis' clout and money he could build a formidable defense, cover his tracks in a hurry, and any mistakes might blow the opportunity to bring all kinds of people to justice. They had to move quickly but judiciously.

Brian Anderberg met them at the airport and took them to a San Antonio hotel.

There was little time for small talk or to get acquainted. Brian Anderberg did joke about the fact that Coach looked a lot better than the last time he saw him, but that was about it. He was very serious, very professional, and his single-mindedness was a reminder of how important this was to the government and to him personally. Turns out he had spent a great deal of time on this, and you could tell by his somber demeanor that his whole career seemed to be tied to this one case. He knew he had to proceed swiftly but carefully. Expeditiously and with caution. Any mistakes and he would be the one held accountable.

Brian hinted about the fact that so far they might have only uncovered the tip of an iceberg. This was much larger than anyone originally had foreseen. Much larger than anyone initially imagined. Including himself. It reached into places that were very fragile and had possible explosive consequences on a national as well as international level.

Coach was so busy thinking about Parker and the game that the description Brian was commencing to draw just wasn't sinking in.

Coach and Joanie barely had time to unpack when they reached the hotel before Sara rejoined them. She informed them that Edward Travis had now promised his full cooperation in the investigation, provided he was granted immunity. He claimed he was innocent; guilty only of being naive. She also told them that Edward Travis was to meet with Lester sometime this morning and tell him everything.

That upset Coach.

His concern, of course, was the fact that Lester was only hours away from having to play in the first round of the Final Four.

Now it was Joanie's turn to get upset.

Sara's cool head prevailed, and she intervened. She explained to Coach that there was a chance Brian could be instructed, by the Bureau, to turn down Travis' immunity request. If that were to happen, they were going to have to arrest Edward Travis. Maybe even this afternoon. And if that were the case, the media would be all over it. The volcano would explode. How would that affect Lester?

Sara informed Coach that Edward Travis told Brian he thought Lester could handle it. Was almost positive he could handle it. That he was a remarkable kid and had no doubts that Lester could still play under the circumstances. He also wanted to show Brian and the government that he was not afraid to tell Lester everything, because ultimately he felt he had nothing to hide. It would be an act of good faith. If he were granted immunity, he would fully cooperate in the investigation no matter how damaging to him or anyone else.

Coach felt Sara was probably right. It made sense. Lester needed to be told. And Coach knew he needed to trust her. She would look out for him. She would look out for Lester.

It was only hours to game time. Somehow Brian had gotten them all tickets. Coach suspected that he wrangled them from Travis himself. He needed to lay down for a while. His head was spinning. He laid down on the hotel bed and tried to read a sports section, hoping his exhaustion would catch up to him and he would be able to fall asleep for just a few minutes.

The sports section's preview of the game was certainly disconcerting. Western Pacific's opponent Kentucky was loaded.

Four of their starters were rumored to be declaring early for the NBA draft. One was a junior, two were sophomores, and one was a freshman. Their fifth starter, a senior, was projected to go in the first round. Maybe the first overall pick. He was a 7'2" 285 pound player from Europe named Otto "Bruiser" Krueger.

The Kentucky Wildcats had made short work of the Duke Blue Devils in the last round.

Kentucky-Duke was a great match-up. It was a rivalry that had a history, but the game wasn't close. Duke got off to a good start and was within 6 at halftime, but the Kentucky Wildcats wore them down and eventually Krueger showed his dominance inside with a series of crushing dunks off some power post moves. When they needed a basket, it went into Bruiser. And he could emphatically deliver.

With Florida's upset over North Carolina, Kentucky was moved up to number one in some of the polls.

The early game would feature the Florida Gators, a team that was making their third visit to the Final Four in the last five years, versus the senior laden Purdue Boilermakers.

Florida was beaten in the championship game the previous year. Three of their starters from the year before had either graduated or declared early for the NBA, but miraculously they had made it back. In a supposedly rebuilding year they had returned by pulling off a stunning upset over the number one seeded and number one ranked North Carolina Tarheels.

The Boilermakers were the Big Ten Champs. They were the first team to go undefeated in that conference in decades. Years ago, one of Bobby Knight's teams at Indiana had accomplished that feat. Purdue only had two blemishes on their record. One was at the hands of Kentucky in a pre-season tournament in Alaska. The other was in a pre-season stunner by the Richmond Spiders. Purdue made it to the Great Eight last year and had everyone back. They were solid, deep, experienced, and a real possibility to win it all.

Western Pacific definitely had the toughest road to the championship. Kentucky was the champion on half the office

180   *Craig Strohm*

pools in America. Western Pacific and Purdue were definitely considered to have an outside chance, but Kentucky was the real deal, and at this point, by far and away the odds-on favorite.

And possibly right about now the Western Pacific point guard, the most important player on their team, a candidate for player of the year, was getting the shock of his life.

Coach was having a hard time falling asleep.

As exhausted as he was, he tossed and turned. Joanie and Sara had gone down to the lobby to get something to eat and check on Brian, whose hotel room had been turned into a command center. The hotel room was dark and quiet, but his mind was racing. He couldn't relax. His mind certainly wasn't buying his theory about this all turning into a funny story a year from now. His idea that it all turns to humor eventually so enjoy the moment, just wasn't washing.

Was I supposed to find Parker? Be careful what you wish for. It all seems unreal. What did you think it would feel like if you found out it was true? Did I really actually believe that Lester was really Parker? Unreal. Now that the truth was about to come out, will it be more harmful than good? "Parker. My little boy. I never meant to hurt you."

I'll never really have my son back anyway. Edward Travis is the only father he has ever known. I'll never really have him back. He's going to probably resent me. Maybe even hate me. I've upset his whole wonderful life. Turned it upside down. "I didn't mean to hurt you Parker. I'm so sorry. Forgive me."

But you are alive. Knowing you are alive, I had to have that. Please understand. I had to have that. My prayers. God's grace. My son. Alive. "Forgive me, Parker. I had to know. Forgive me."

When Joanie and Sara returned with Brian an hour later, they found Coach fast asleep. They had to wake him up.

Brian gave Coach an abbreviated update. He quickly described the direction the investigation was now heading.

All that Edward Travis had offered so far was that he admitted adopting from an agency in San Diego. Most of the arrangements were not made by him, but by people he hired. He didn't ask questions and assumed everything was on the up and up. And that, primarily, was the extent of what he was willing to offer unless he was granted his immunity from any prosecution.

Brian mentioned the fact that even before Edward Travis' name came up, the agency was already investigating various adoption agencies in Southern California, one of which was a seamy operation they had heard of located in the San Diego area. These agencies were not registered with the state or federal governments and quite possibly were headquartered down in Mexico. He said he couldn't stress enough the importance of this particular case in allowing them to uncover a dirty and awful business that might be sweeping the country. There were hints that illegal adoption schemes were becoming big business in America. Even signs of child slavery kidnapping rackets were beginning to turn up, and not just in third-world countries, but in the good old USA. There was a whole series of mysterious disappearances all across the nation that might be linked to this filthy business growing the world over.

Brian told Coach that a year ago he had been put in charge of the Bureau's investigation into the suspected adoption scandals.

All his efforts for an entire year had been spent on this one investigation. He uncovered very little hard evidence. He detected its existence, knew it was there and possible growing, but up until now he had very little to go on. Edward Travis, he said, could be the key to unlocking the whole thing. He could be the key to uncovering a whole West Coast pipeline of suspected child abductions. The top directors at the FBI were meeting right now to consider Edward Travis' request by his lawyers; full cooperation for a get out of jail free card. He would receive the Bureau's answer tonight, possibly sometime after the game.

Brian arranged for a car to pick them up for the game.

They all left the room together and got on the elevator. Joanie was very quiet. Ever since that morning on the backyard deck she had been very reluctant to leave Coach's side. She held his hand, or she hung on to his arm. It felt a little like old times. It felt good. Earlier it dawned on Coach that Joanie hadn't seen Parker yet, not up close and in person anyway. She had only seen the picture on the cover of *Sports Illustrated*, which was over a month ago, and she barely even glanced at it before flinging it across the room.

He had already survived the shock. Now it was her turn.

She was nervous. Tense.

So was he.

Kentucky's starting five looked like an NBA team. They were massive.

And they were almost as old as a professional team.

The basketball team at Kentucky had become somewhat of a renegade program since Rick Pitino and Tubby Smith left for the NBA. Kentucky became the target of several NCAA investigations. Nothing had been proven, however, and there were no sanctions or penalties handed down. Not yet. They had accumulated a questionable and diverse collection of talent that included black-top players, street ballers, country sharpshooters and European Olympians.

They won back to back league championships and finished ranked in the top ten the past two seasons. Last year a miraculous half court buzzer beater by St. Johns kept them from advancing to the Final Four.

Their starting five included a transfer from Louisville who was expelled from the school when he was arrested for burglarizing another student's apartment. He had to sit out a year before becoming eligible at Kentucky. He was now listed as a junior. Their two sophomore starters were both from an East Coast private academy that was nothing more than a basketball factory: a holding tank for players until they became eligible or passed the SAT. The lone freshman was a red shirt, the youngest of the starters. He had turned twenty-one in February. All of them were basketball prodigies, pampered by shoe companies since grade school. Veterans of all-star AAU teams that played all summer and traveled everywhere around the USA and Europe. They were given cars and cash all through high school by AAU benefactors. Even their families benefited from their basketball abilities. New homes. New jobs. All seemingly legal as shoe companies like Nike and Adidas continually found ways to get around NCAA regulations. A Kentucky connection was the latest program benefiting the most from its ties with some shady characters who ran the grass-roots programs for these AAU all-star shoe company teams.

And then there was Otto "Bruiser" Krueger.

He transferred from a university in Germany. He was a twenty-four-year-old gigantic who played as if he disagreed with everything. Thought to be much heavier than his listed weight, he twice played on Germany's Olympic team starting at the age of sixteen. He already had a spot reserved for him in the next Olympics. He lacked the speed and athleticism of the other four starters, but he was a huge presence in the paint. A great shot blocker with good hands and an array of post moves with a soft touch. Some sportswriters were calling him the next Shaquille O'Neal. Shaquille was the mammoth in the middle during the Los Angeles Laker resurgence under Coach Phil Jackson. Western Pacific's center would be giving up four inches and at least forty pounds to Krueger.

The four of them, Joanie, Coach, Sara, and Brian, had managed to end up with good seats.

They sat together thirty rows up directly across from the Western Pacific bench. Across the arena, almost at the same level, was Edward Travis. Brian said the man he was presently sitting next to was his well known lead attorney. Edward Travis' wife was not present. According to Brian, Rebecca and Edward were rumored to have had a little spat the night before, and she left for LA to pack. Seems she was having a hard time dealing with the impending embarrassment. Hearsay was, they were finished. She was leaving him.

I guess Parker is dealing with that too! Didn't he think that she was his mother? Mother! Wow! Now Parker has that to think about that too. How is he supposed to deal with that and play basketball? Right! This is too much. This could be a disaster. A complete disaster.

Out on the floor Florida was chasing Purdue around trying to commit fouls.

They were trying to get Purdue to miss free-throws so they could cut into their seven point lead with under a minute to go. Purdue wasn't cooperating. They were making the free-throws and widening the margin. It was Purdue by 12 as the buzzer sounded. The Boilermakers were heading to the championship for the first time in over twenty-five years.

During the Western Pacific-Kentucky warm-ups, like Joanie, Coach couldn't keep his eyes off of Parker.

Joanie clung to Coach.

She couldn't hold back the tears that were persistently welling up in her eyes. Coach could relate. It was almost impossible to come to terms with the realization that this was really happening. It was certainly more than one person could possibly comprehend. The fact that he actually believed for the last couple of months that Lester could be Parker did not even come close to preparing him for the actual impact of the whole thing. It was overwhelming. Staggering. This was a whole new ball game.

You actually believe there might be life on other planets. And then you see a UFO. You meet an alien. Whole new ball game!

Their relatively normal, quiet and obscure life was about to become a national media phenomena. A three-ring circus.

Parker was alive. Parker was back.

Coach broke a period of silence by bringing up Michelle. He suggested, once again, they call her. This time Joanie had no objections. No reservations. She closed her eyes and nodded in agreement. Now she felt guilty.

Coach said he would call as soon as they got back to the hotel and make the travel arrangements for Michelle and her husband.

The magnitude, the surrealness of the whole thing had now completely engulfed Joanie. She was transfixed by Parker. Watching him so intently as he went through pregame warm-ups. To conceive that their son, their son, had been saved, rescued, and delivered back to them.

A miracle.

And now she knew. It was true. It was all true. Coach didn't have to ask what she was thinking.

He knew. He had felt it too. Still did.

There could be no doubts now. Not for Joanie. It no longer required faith, like it had so long for Coach. A mother knows her own son.

And Joanie knew. She was watching her child.

Coach put his arm around her shoulders and they held on to each other tight. Originally, Coach had to go it alone. Weathered the storm by himself. He barely survived . No need for Joanie to have to. She had him. And always would.

They watched their son together like proud and satisfied parents.

Does Parker know who I am now? Does he now know that he is the son of old Coach Peterson? That I'm his real father? How is he ever going to be able to play in this game? Was telling him the right thing? If they lose this game, will Parker blame me? He's going to blame me.

I must surrender this! Have to surrender this. But its so hard. I want to protect this. Protect him. Keep this off limits. But, I have to give this up. Like everything else. I have to give this up. Have to put this in God's hands. His hands. His plan. Have faith! Have faith! It will be all right!

It was time for the team introductions.

The next time Lester Travis is introduced as a player it might be as Parker Peterson. Parker Peterson!

Coach suddenly had juice. Electrification. It had returned.

Boy, it's been awhile. The game. The game. It's game time! This is big! Very big!

His head began to pound. Clammy hands. Underarm sweat races. His heart thumping away as his blood pressure climbed. Tension mounting. Soaring. It had been a long time since he felt this way, but he recognized it. He was feeling that pressure. The pressure to win a basketball game.

How can this feel good? But it does. Kinda sick really. How can I miss this? But I do! I really do!

"The Star Spangled Banner" began and Coach had a flash-back.
A flashback to one of his old pre-game routines.
At the beginning of every game he coached when the Star Spangled Banner was played he would close his eyes and think back to where he came from. Back to where it all started. His life. His boyhood. He would picture the little house on Forest Avenue back in Wisconsin. The one back in Twin Rivers that he grew up in. So small. Typical really. Midwestern. A factory town.

He would think about his parents. He would recall his two sisters and the three of them struggling to come of age. The things they went through to survive as a family. The striving. A life so filled with uncertainties.

His parents worked hard. Sometimes at two different jobs just to make ends meet. They didn't have much, but they had enough. And they had things that money can't buy. His parents had sacrificed much for them. And the love. The love they had for him, and his two sisters. And so proud. How proud they were of them. And their devotion to each other. No matter how rough it got or how much they might disagree, their devotion was unbending. Just like their faith. Unyielding and inflexible. He thought about it all.

Then, while the song was still playing, he would say a prayer. He would say a prayer thanking the Lord for his blessings.

He would thank the Lord for everything. The good and the bad. The ups and the downs. The victories and the defeats. The successes and the failures. The celebrations and the disappointments. His journey. These were part of everything he was.

Think about back home. His start. That's where he got his strength. His land. His people. His history. That's where the magic came from. It humbled him. And it made him eternally grateful.

Now, standing in front of his seat in an unexpected place at this totally unexpected point in time, holding tight to Joanie's hand, he closed his eyes again.

And like he did so many times before, for so many years, before so many games, while the "Star Spangled Banner" played. . . .

He remembered.
And he said his prayer.

CHAPTER TWENTY

APRIL 3, 2004

WESTERN PACIFIC VS. KENTUCKY

ALAMODOME

SAN ANTONIO

Kentucky controlled the tip.

On the first possession Western Pacific was beat on the baseline. The Wildcat forward dished to Otto "Bruiser" Krueger and he two-handed power dunked.

He was fouled.

He made the free-throw.

He would finish with 29 points, including ten field goals, most of which would be dunks. He was 9 of 12 from the free-throw line. During the entire game, Western Pacific had no answer for Bruiser.

The Pirates turned the ball over on their first offensive possession. Kentucky scored again on penetration and a pass to Krueger.

Parker missed a three and Kentucky ran with the long rebound. Parker gave chase, but in his attempt to block the layup he committed a foul.

The layup was good.

So was the foul shot.

Western Pacific time-out.
Kentucky 8 Western Pacific 0.

Western Pacific's Coach Schmidt would make his first adjustment.

No more help on the drive by the post defenders. Sag off the perimeter players and surround Bruiser. Make any penetrater by Kentucky have to finish or force them to beat you from the outside. If the ball did get into Bruiser on the block, then double, triple, cripple, whatever it took, but don't let him go up with it. Make someone else on Kentucky beat you. Find out what kind of passer Krueger is.

Parker hit a three and the Pirates were finally on the board.

He came off a point to wing screen and his man was forced to cheat under. Parker faded back to the trey line, caught and fired a fall away jump shot.

It was a bomb really. Long range. Forced. Lucky.

Kentucky was doing a great job making it tough for Parker to get the ball. One of the things Western Pacific was great at was fast breaking after the other team scored. The Wildcats were double teaming Parker after they scored, forcing the Pirates to bring the ball up and start their offense with someone else besides Parker.

It was slowing them down. Krueger was sticking around to harass any defensive rebounds the Pirates got, also making it difficult to get a quick outlet to Parker and start any fast transition after a Kentucky miss. To see Kentucky with all their talent executing a game plan was scary.

After Parker's basket, Western Pacific finally had the opportunity to press. It didn't force a turnover, but you could tell the Wildcats were much more tentative on their attack.

It was obvious. Western Pacific needed the press to win. They needed the pressure on Kentucky, they needed the shot clock to reduce their offensive possession time. With ample shot clock time it was just too easy to get Bruiser involved.

The opportunity for WPU to press, however, was only there if they could score. And the opportunity wasn't occurring often enough.

For the next ten minutes the margin bounced between 5 and 8. Western Pacific was unable to catch them, unable to make a run. With eight minutes to go in the half, Parker was called for a reaching foul. It was not an obvious foul. Phantom call. He might have even had all ball.
He complained to the official.
The Kentucky guard got in Parker's face. Talked some trash.
Parker gave him a shove!
Technical foul! On Parker!

It was so uncharacteristic of Parker.
He was known as one of the most composed and focused players in the country. His attitude, his composure and maturity was one of the main subjects in the article that appeared in *Sports Illustrated.*
The article had gone on and on about how he was "old school." No trash. No chest thumping. Never over celebrated. Always in control. Always acted like he'd been there before.
He was quiet confidence personified. The article compared him to a lion who waits patiently, relaxing, dozing, in the shade on the Serengeti Plains. In a single second he could be up running, chasing down his prey. Moments later, back lying down in the cool of the shade tree. Licking his paws.
Western Pacific fans were shocked. The media was shocked. Even his teammates were caught off guard and had not immediately intervened between him and the Kentucky guard. Never saw it coming.
It was all the Wildcat fans needed. They smelled blood and they were all standing and pointing at Parker.
"You, you, you. . . ."
Most of the sportswriters believed that Western Pacific was a much bigger obstacle than Purdue would be if Kentucky were

to win the championship. Kentucky fans knew it too. And now they had the Pirates on the ropes. They had an 8 point lead and Western Pacific's best player had to go to the bench. They were frustrated and in foul trouble.

The Wildcats took advantage of the confusion.

Over the last 8 minutes until halftime Kentucky out-scored Western Pacific 20 to 7.

And after every basket they celebrated back down the floor. Dancing. Pointing to each other. Hooting and hollering. Playing to the crowd and the cameras.

The Kentucky players jumped into each others arms when the halftime buzzer sounded.

Kentucky led 46-25.

It was obvious to Coach that Parker's game was indeed being affected by the recent events in his life. Who wouldn't be?

Parker was playing angry.

Not allowing the game to come to him. Forcing everything. Offensively and defensively. No flow. No rhythm.

Offensively, he had five points. The one basket he made, the three pointer, was forced, just like his other attempts. He was trying to get involved, trying to give his team a lift, but it was not coming in the course of the offensive flow. One basket, 2 free-throws, foul trouble. That was the extent of his contribution.

Defensively he was also showing his agitation. Impatience. He was overly aggressive. Over anxious. Twice he was beat on reaches trying to take the ball away from his man off the dribble. Playing the dribble instead of the man. On occasion, during the Pirate press, he rotated too early and left his own man open for an easy basket.

The Pirates had never had to play a tough one without Parker, and they didn't quite know what to do. Nobody stepped up, nobody took control.

Coach didn't feel like talking. He couldn't help but think that the outcome of this game had been turned by the events that were transpiring behind the scenes. And of course he wanted to blame himself.

"Great job, Dad! You cost me the National Championship! What did you say your name was? Dirt bag?"

Over the last 5 minutes of the half, the four of them sitting together in the stands had ceased any running commentary, other than some grunts and groans.

Brian was the first to speak.

"Wow, doesn't look good." He stood up and stretched. "I think I could use a beer. There's got to be a bar in here somewhere. Anybody want to join me? I'm buying."

"I'll join you," it was Sara getting up from her seat now. "Maybe it'll change our luck. I remember you being so superstitious Coach. Same tie. Same pants. Picking up pennies all the time. Change one thing, change everything, you used to say. Well, I'm going with Brian to change my attitude. Maybe that'll help. Care to join us? Joanie? Coach?"

"I don't think today would be a good day for me to start drinking again. I might not ever stop. I could use a dog and a coke though," Coach said as he also slowly got to his feet. "What about you, honey? Do you want to go with Sara and Brian? Or join me? I can fetch you something if you want me to."

Joanie looked numb. Consumed. Spent. And now she looked concerned that Coach was considering leaving her to go get a hot-dog. Coach had never seen her so fragile. She was always so independent. Strong. Defiant. If you even so much as hinted at a weakness, you might pay for it.

Joanie managed to catch herself just in time. No chinks in the armor! "Maybe some water. Get me a bottle of water if they have one. It's getting so hot in here," she said forcing a smile.

Coach was almost relieved.

He could be alone. Wanted to be alone. If not, just for a few minutes. He needed to stand. To walk. And he didn't feel like talking. He was too nervous. He was drenched with sweat. It was almost ready to come through the sweater he was wearing. He was soaked, and he knew it wasn't from the heat in the arena.

If they somehow could have won this game. The championship game wouldn't have mattered. Parker would not have held me responsible for that one. It was two days away. He would have had time. Time. Time to adjust to the whole thing. This game was the one. It doesn't look good. Doesn't look good. The timing. It was terrible. I could have at least waited. We should have waited.

Coach was back in his seat next to Joanie and Sara finishing a hot-dog when Brian returned. Sara had returned by herself just moments before Brian's arrival.

Coach felt compelled to choke down the dog because he used that for his excuse to get up and move around. He knew it was the wrong thing to do knowing just how nervous he was. He certainly wasn't the least bit hungry. He used the hot-dog trip to try and relieve some anxiety and now it allowed his stomach to join in on his overall discomfort.

Sara was sitting next to Joanie.

Coach was on one end next to Joanie; Brian was on the other end sitting on the aisle. Brian leaned around Sara to make sure that Coach and Joanie could hear.

"Well, I called Washington. They're going to give Travis what he wants. Immunity. They think it's in our best interest. Star witness I guess. Ironic, huh? Travis gets to be a star. I'll be meeting with Travis' and his lawyers first thing in the morning. They've appointed me head of the task force. It'll be in place by Monday. We're of course going to start by my grilling Travis. Sara, I was wondering if you would help me with the investigation? Join the task force and help me with Travis' interrogation tomorrow? If you would? I've already cleared it with the Bureau. You'd be great. I could really use your help."

Sara was quick to respond.

"I don't think you want me on the thing. Cuz I think they should hang the SOB."

Joanie was quick to agree. "I'm with you, Sara."

Coach put his two cents in. "Yeah, but maybe it's for the best. Get to the bottom of the whole thing. Fast."

"But, Coach," it was Sara again. "What if it turns out this thing is a whole lot more sophisticated than we all thought? Brian knows. He knows. This thing might have been planned, Coach. You may as well know the whole truth. Coach, it might not have been random. The whole thing. The kidnapping. Abduction. The adoption. There's a chance it's a mail order operation, Coach. What if it turns out you popped up on someone's computer? You and Parker. Because some nut case. . . ."

Brian interrupted. "Hold on, Sara. We don't know if anything like that is true. And if it turns out it is, Travis might be the only guy who could crack the whole thing open. And in a hurry."

"I don't care," said Sara. "Just think about it. The thought of some geek movie maker with a lot of money ordering and then paying for a kid who he thought might turn out to be a jock. What does he do if it doesn't turn out the way he had hoped? Throw him away? It's sick. Sick!"

All Joanie could do was stare at both Brian and Sara. Chilled. Goose bumps. Chicken skin. Shock.

Coach spoke. "Why haven't you told us this before? Why did you wait till now?"

"Well, we don't have much to go on yet," Brian answered. "At first it seemed too bizarre to even imagine. It was a pretty radical theory. But then we studied some of the missing children around the country. Well, we found they were special children from special parents. All around the same age. They were disappearing. No traces. No bodies found in shallow graves."

Now it was Sara's turn again. "Coach, it could be that Parker wasn't just some random spontaneous snatching. You might have been followed. Stalked. Once you were targeted you probably couldn't have avoided it. Not in this country. Not in any country in the world. If not the mall, then preschool or the supermarket. From your front lawn. There's a good chance this was not done by just some crackpot. This was planned by professionals. It's pretty sick to even imagine this being true. But the fact is, it might be."

Joanie was dumbfounded. Coach was speechless too.

"Well, Sara could be right," Brian sighed. "At first it just seemed way too improbable. Much too sick, like Sara said. Then things began to line up. The ages. An age when a kid could still forget his past. The age when they could determine if the kid was going to be healthy. Medical records were in place. They could tell what they were going to look like. Computer enhancement. Use computer projections. They could tell if there would be enough similarities to the new parents so no suspicions would be raised. It's all so easy to fabricate, forge, and produce records these days. It's a joke. Think about it. No muss. No fuss. No diapers. No sleepless nights. Ready for the nanny. Ordered and delivered. Ready for you to become part of the youth soccer league in your community. Sara's right. It's all very sick. Very sick."

Joanie started to cry. Coach didn't notice at first, but he was now holding her. His arm was tight around her shoulders.

"I'm sorry. I'm so sorry," Sara was having a tough time talking too." She was wiping her eyes on the sleeve of her jacket "That is why I think they should hang the son of a bitch. Steal someone's kid. They should castrate the bastard."

Joanie leaned her face on Coach's shoulder.

Brian, Sara, and Coach now stared silently down at the arena floor as the two teams returned to the court for the second half.

Western Pacific ripped off the first 8 points.

Two threes by Parker.

One of them came off a long outlet in which he passed up a possible driving layup and pulled up for a trey. A running leaner.

Net.
Time-out Kentucky.

Parker looked possessed.
For the next 17 minutes Parker Peterson dominated the game. Simply took it over.

In the first half he looked almost ordinary. Just another solid college player
Another Indian. Part of the tribe.
In the second half he demonstrated what everyone was talking about.

That special ability to rise above the rest, that elite plateau that is inhabited by the greatest of the greats. Capable of extraordinary exploits, these impeccable warriors possess a will that enables them to transcend what is thought to be possible. The impossible is conceived, and then it is accomplished. The statures of these magicians and their wizardry are what legends are built on.

Even their fiercest enemies stand in awe and cannot help but offer their adulation. Just like the rest of us bystanders, they too pay homage, honor, and become members of the secret admiration society. The perfection they present is preserved in us forever. Their performance is a pure presence, not some platonic ideal.

They are not necessarily solo assailants either, waging gorilla warfare. Never solitary snipers crouching in the jungle. Never cold blooded murderers.

They are noble. Chivalrous. Consummate team combatants.

Braves.

They possess medicine so powerful it has the strength to enhance everyone's craving to converge into a perfect confluence. A sacred hoop. At the center, complete effort, effulgent execution.

Their selfless combativeness creates orchestration. It becomes a choreographed dance. A theatrical production. All players able to move together as one with precision and timing. They are the performances that become almost mythological. They are the Birds, the MJ's, the Magics. Because of their peerless ability to play as if their very life depended on it, their teams become invincible.

Fight as you may, at some point you accept your fate and sing your death song.

Nobody could match Parker's ferocity.

Nobody could match his fire. His determination and sense of desperation. His relentless energy. As his confidence grew so did his imagination. And he began to execute spectacular moves that brought the crowd to its feet.

With 7 minutes to go, Western Pacific tied the game.

They had erased a 20 point deficit.

Parker was on the free-throw line after having been mauled by Bruiser. Krueger was trailing yet another Pirate fastbreak; Parker stopped and pulled up for a three-point attempt, and out of frustration Bruiser gave him a forearm to the back. Parker went sprawling into the paint but jumped back up immediately and went to the free-throw line for his three shots. It was Krueger's 4th foul, and another nail in Kentucky's coffin.

Brian, Sara, and Coach were now becoming boisterous fans. All felt an incredible sense of relief. Joanie was a little more conservative, but she was beginning to enjoy herself too. Brian, Sara, and Coach were up cheering along with the Pirate fans. They were on their feet, clapping, yelling, laughing, high fiving.

"I can't believe this. This has to be some kind of a record," said Brian.

"Awesome! Totally awesome!" said Sara excitedly. "Well, there is no doubt in my mind. That's your kid, Coach! He has to be related to you. He's a total gunner. I know. I've played with you, Coach," Sara leaned over and laughed as she teased Coach.

"You're right, Sara. I think we can use this game tape as the final proof. Forget about all that DNA stuff!" Coach was smiling and nodding in agreement. But he still secretly held some reservations about the final outcome. He had been involved in some unusual endings to too many basketball games over the years, and he knew enough not to be putting this one prematurely in the bank. It was looking a whole lot better; however, the game had definitely changed, and in Coach's experience very few teams survived such a tremendous and devastating shift in momentum.

Kentucky was collapsing. A house of cards.

They were still pointing fingers, but it wasn't to recognize "Nice pass bro, " it was more like "Whose man was that?"

Western Pacific had gone to a five guard offense. Instead of trying to match the Wildcat size, they spread the floor and forced Bruiser away from the basket. It opened up the driving lanes and backdoor cuts. If Kentucky tried to cheat and sag to help, the Pirates were making them pay with three-pointers.

Kentucky's offense was reduced to one on one, with the other four players standing around. It started to look like an NBA offense. They stopped moving to get open and they stopped setting screens to help out teammates.

Western Pacific was getting too much help from their pressure half court defense to allow any one Kentucky player to take over. Their Coach was exasperated, and there were heated exchanges between him and players during time-outs. Kentucky was in a full panic mode.

Now that Western Pacific was scoring consistently, the press began to fatigue Kentucky.

Kentucky turnover's were mounting.

Krueger trailed behind almost every Pirate possession. At the three minute mark, and Western Pacific ahead by 5, he committed his 5th foul. He appeared exhausted and had had enough.

Still Coach was nervous.

"Coach, will you relax," Sara teased some more. "Kentucky is dead. Look at them. They're hanging on to their skirts on the free-throw line. It looked like old Bruiser was relieved to hit the bench. Stick a fork in 'em Coach. Were going to the Final."

"Hey, there's three minutes left," Coach responded.

"Yeah, three minutes, and it's going to get worse," Brian's added analysis. "Sara's right, Coach. Put it in the books. This one is over."

Sara was right. The final minutes were more of the same. Kentucky couldn't find a way to score without Bruiser, and Western Pacific closed it out from the free-throw line.

Western Pacific didn't have a defensive answer for Otto "Bruiser" Krueger. But Kentucky didn't have one for Parker Peterson either.

He finished with 33 points, 11 assists, 6 rebounds, 4 steals. He was a perfect 9 for 9 from the line.

The whole country had just witnessed one of the grittiest and inspiring performances in the history of the NCAA tournament.

What they didn't know was that Parker did it playing in a great deal of pain.

But they were only a few days away from finding out the whole remarkable story.

The truth was coming. The truth was on its way.

Joanie and Coach remained in their seats a long time after most of the arena had emptied.

They watched Parker get interviewed on TV. Then some of his teammates. Then Edward Travis.

They didn't speak much, just stared down at the floor watching the post game wrap-up. Both, however, were wondering about the same things.

What's it going to be like? What am I going to say? Strange thing to be terrified of meeting your own son. When's it going to happen? Tomorrow? Monday? It's going to be soon. What am I going to say. Gotta think about that. What do you say?

Brian and Sara had left to check in with their superiors. Joanie and Coach were sitting in an almost empty arena when they finally returned.

Brian came down the row of seats behind them and hopped over the empty seat next to Coach and flopped down. "He wants to meet with you, Coach. Tomorrow."

Coach turned to look at Brian.

"Tomorrow, Coach," Brian continued. "Edward Travis wants to meet you. Tomorrow. Both of you. Joanie and you."

Coach and Joanie exchanged a glance, and both simultaneously nodded while turning back toward the arena floor. Allowing what Brian just said to sink in. There wasn't really a need to say anything. They were both thinking the same thing. Joanie squeezed his hand a little tighter.

Tomorrow. Tomorrow.

"What about Parker?" Coach suddenly asked Brian, while still staring down at the court.

"Soon, Coach. Soon," answered Brian.

CHAPTER TWENTY-ONE

APRIL 4, 2004

SUNDAY AFTERNOON

SAN ANTONIO

EMBASSY SUITES

"He's your son now, Mr. Peterson."
It was Edward Travis speaking.

They were in a hotel suite situated high above the pictur-esque Paseo Del Rio, better known as the River Walk, in down-town San Antonio. Although Edward Travis had spent most of the previous night meeting with his attorneys and most of the morning with Brian and Sara, Travis desperately wanted to meet Joanie and Coach.
Coach didn't expect Travis to look this young.
There was always some distance between him and Travis when he saw him at the arenas or in the parking lot that night in Phoenix. Not a whole lot of distance, but some. Enough that he hadn't really gotten a good look at him. Up close now he thought he looked so much younger than he did.

Jeez, Coach. What do you expect? He's what? Forty-eight? You're going to be sixty in June. Get a grip!

There were countless other differences too. Travis was Armani. Rolex. Italian shoes. He was fit and tanned. Manicured and gelled. Although he looked a little jagged and spent, like they all did at this point, he was Southern California. Hollywood. A stark contrast to Coach. Coach was Dockers. Polo shirt. Dirty running shoes. In need of a haircut.

Coach felt old. Self-conscious.

"Be careful what you say, Ed," Travis' attorney was cautioning him.

Edward Travis had two attorneys present. One of them was the attorney who sat next to Travis at the game Saturday night. Brian pointed out that he was a well known lawyer who had been known to appear on various talk shows from time to time, like Geraldo Rivera, giving his opinion and debating legal issues connected to a whole assortment of current litigation.

Travis' two lawyers sat together on a small couch across a coffee table from Joanie and Coach who were also sitting together on a couch. In chairs on opposite ends of Joanie and Coach's couch sat Brian and Sara. The two sides facing each other. Peterson vs. Travis. The coffee table was covered with folders and papers and two digital recorders. Each set of attorneys was recording the proceeding.

The only one who presently stood was Edward Travis. He was moving around the room as he talked. He was hyperactive. Spoke very fast and was very animated. Coach began to wonder if he was one of those unable to ever really relax. The kind of person whose loquacious behavior could make a rock nervous.

"Shut up, Bill," Travis snapped. "Aren't we here for Lester? Or, I suppose, I should start calling him Parker. Isn't this about him? What's good for him? Aren't we here for the truth? I adopted a stolen child." His frankness was making Joanie and Coach cringe. "I, unknowingly of course, participated in the kidnapping of a child."

"Be careful, Ed. Please. Be careful," the Travis attorney was interrupting again.

Travis continued, "I wanted a son. I married a woman who decided after we were married she didn't want to compromise herself physically to have children. So, what did I do? I went and bought one. And then I created a big lie to go along with it."

"Maybe we should take a break?" Travis' lawyer again.

"Bill, if you interrupt me one more time," Travis said abruptly pointing his finger at his attorney. "You just don't get it. I don't care. I really don't care. I'm ashamed. I'm humiliated. My career might very well be over. I'm probably ruined. But I'm no longer going to live with this. This lie. Now out of respect for these people, I've got to try and make this thing right." He turned to look at Joanie and Coach and then back to his attorneys. "Please. Please. Let me finish!"

Coach believed there was some truth to what he was saying. It was all very theatrical, of course. Travis was over acting. He was trying to save his skin, but Coach wanted to believe it was somewhat sincere. He wasn't sure if Joanie was buying it. He knew that he was more naive than Joanie, or more naive than most people in general. Always has been. He tended to trust people. Even though Brian and Sara warned both Joanie and him that they found Edward Travis very slick, very, very, smart, artfully manipulative, possessing an overwhelming and convincing dramatic flare, Coach still wanted to believe him.

Edward Travis continued, "It seemed so innocent at the time. I trusted the people who worked for me. It's easy, they said. You want to have a son? No problem. There are plenty of unwanted children out there. I admit one thing. I was suspicious. But you see, I had just about everything a man could ever want. Everything. But it wasn't enough. I wanted a son. I admit I'm guilty of that. After all, it was an unwanted child. Right? What's the difference if I make it look like my own? Call it vanity. The people that work for me assured me it was no big deal. No one will care. You're doing something good here, they said. We'll take care of it, they said. I, of course, was too busy to get involved myself. So, I gave the go ahead. Go ahead. Look into the possibilities. Do the research. Take care of the paper work."

Brian and Sara sat passively while Travis spoke. They had heard most of the same story that morning. They spent hours before noon grilling him. Coach knew what they were thinking. He could feel it. They weren't buying it. They were wishing they could have gotten a chance to prosecute Travis. They felt there were too many holes in his story. Inconsistencies. Too many parts left out. Certain areas avoided. The whole fabrication of trying to turn Parker into his real son. They knew there was a smoking gun somewhere, and they knew they were going to find it with or without Travis. He was guilty. They both saw Travis as too much of a hands-on guy not to have masterminded or at least been aware of the extent of the elaborate counterfeit conception and its legal ramifications. He knew. Brian saw Travis as the classic control freak. An aggressive, dominating personality in which a dreadful fear of failure keeps him from delegating. The up-side for Brian was that he knew that because of Travis' terrifying feeling of being out of control, he would give up anyone of his associates and step over anyone who might be in his way in his attempt to save himself.

It especially unnerved Brian and Sara that many of the people in this country who were getting rich felt like that along with their new found wealth, they also acquired an exemption from the laws of the land. That many people today equated being busy with being exceptional and consequential.

But the Bureau had decided that whatever they could get from Travis would be far more beneficial than a lengthy investigation and his attempted prosecution. Give Travis some rope, and he might not be able to hang himself, but he would be willing to hang a lot of others. Besides, they needed to get right to the bottom. And fast. Speed was of the essence. Even though they were already trying their hardest to safeguard Travis, to isolate him, they understood that security and confidentiality were now absent in America. Privacy? Long gone. There would be leaks, if there weren't already. Brian agreed with the Bureau that the entire syndicate needed to be ambushed within the next two days, or it would be impossible to find these people.

In Travis' case, justice might not be served, but putting an end to this whole abduction/adoption business in the United States and beyond had to be their prime objective.

Travis wouldn't go to prison, but he would be forced to live with the lie. Publicly. And to live with the consequences. Besides, Brian figured there were other ways to make Travis pay for his crimes. He could make his life a living hell if he wanted to. The legal system in America today was too slow, too deliberate, a quagmire, but the government was still a powerful entity.

Edward Travis continued, "As time went on, I grew to love that little boy. Loved him more than life itself. I tried to convince myself he was an abandoned child. A forgotten child that I was now providing a good home. But as time went on, I grew even more suspicious. He was so incredibly special. And I don't mean the athletic ability either. He was just so special. So smart. So . . . everything. I couldn't turn back. How could I turn back? I was terrified to even ask questions. Afraid of what I might find out. The truth? That might have been suicide opening myself up to all sorts of things. Blackmail. Payoffs. Prison. Looking back, of course, I wish I had. The guilt? The distrust? The paranoia? It continued to grow. At times it was unbearable. Excruciating. I was living a lie. One big shameful and disgusting lie. The ramifications just got larger and larger and more and more out of control. My wife? At first no big deal. Life in the fast lane. But eventually it destroyed whatever we had. Other people? People who worked for me? Some of them knew the truth or were suspect. I was constantly worried one of them would give me up. My relationship with them . . . I was already being extorted. Compromised. Financially. Artistically. You name it. So much paranoia. Anxiety. Fear. If it gets out, I'm finished. Everything I built. Everything I owned. I knew it could all come crashing down in an instant. As sick as it sounds, I couldn't give it up. Just couldn't. The money. The power. And most of all? Most of all . . . Lester. I couldn't even imagine giving him up. No way. He became worth the risk of losing everything. I just couldn't do it. No way. I had to try and continue to live with it."

Edward Travis sat down in a chair next to his lawyers, slumped over, and put his face in his hands. The room was silent. All assuming the same posture. Follow the leader. Monkey see. Simon says. Heads down, staring at the floor. Unable to look at each other. Joanie held Coach's hand in her lap, and together they also stared down at their feet.

When Travis looked up, tears were rolling down his face. "Mr. and Mrs. Peterson, I'm guilty. I'm guilty of being a greedy, selfish, pathetic egomaniac. I'm not worthy of being anyone's father, let alone Lester's. I can't imagine how you must have suffered. But I assure you, I'll do everything in my power to try and make this up to you. And to Lester. Everything. How can I make this right?" He stopped to compose himself before continuing. "If I had known this was going to be a kidnapping . . . an abduction. If I knowingly had been apart of that, I would gladly go to jail. I would deserve jail. Deserve to rot there. But I'm innocent of that. I'm innocent of being a part of that."

Edward Travis was begging for his life. At the same instant everyone in the room realized it. He was begging for his life, and he was begging for forgiveness that could only come from Joanie and Coach.

There was something so pathetic, so sad, about him. This famous rich movie producer, who thought he had everything, was now pleading for mercy from two people whose plight his condescending arrogance ordinarily would have disregarded along with other strangers along a street. He was a man who thought he was vital, only to discover that his ruthless ambition and intense quest for materialism had depleted him of all spiritual nourishment. Left him hollow. He had been seduced by the primitive and hedonistic assumption that commodities can produce happiness and health, only to be left hungry, starving and suffering from malnutrition of the soul. The pursuit of power, wealth, and prestige had only left him deficient, and unprotected from the degenerative moral decay.

Coach was staring down at the coffee table. An uncomfortable silence had now settled on the proceedings. Everyone in the room not quite sure where to go next. Coach was confused. Conscientious. Brian and Sara had cautioned both Joanie and Coach not to be compromised by Travis' persuasive abilities, had warned them both, repeatedly, of his talent for manipulation and deception. Coach couldn't help it. If they were hiring for hate, Coach could put together a pretty good resume. No one would ever question his qualifications. But he felt some sympathy. Sympathy. Maybe, once again, it was his stubborn sense of morality, and maybe it was a lifetime spent teaching, a job that demanded compassion, despite constant exploitation.

Is this Hollywood? One big act? Does he actually think that I believe this? That I can forgive him? He stole my son! He had the crap beat out of me. Acting? One big act. Who does he think I am? But. Does it matter? When you think about it? Does it really matter?

"I want to see my son." It was Coach who suddenly broke the silence. His abruptness surprised him. "I want to see my son," he repeated. It came out of nowhere. It was loud, absolute and powerful. Coach hadn't said a single word up to that point. His voice was commanding. It startled the group and demanded everyone come to attention. A smile came over Sara's face; she recognized that voice. All eyes were on him now. He slowly got to his feet and let go of Joanie's hand.

Coach spoke slowly and deliberately, "I don't know if I'll ever have my son back. I do know that he deserves the truth. The truth must be told. He deserves that. Mr. Travis, I don't know what to believe. I'm not sure at this point I really care. I want the pain to go away. I want the suffering to stop. I don't know where this will all end. But I do know that it has to begin with forgiveness."

Brian, Sara, and Joanie looked bewildered. Perplexed. They all were of the same opinion. The only thing Edward Travis deserved was prison. For life. He didn't deserve anything else, let alone Coach's forgiveness.

Edward Travis stood up and faced Coach. Coach was much older looking than Travis, but even at his age, he stood at least six or seven inches taller. Standing this close, Travis was forced to tilt his head back to look up at Coach's face.

For the last twenty-five years, every room Travis entered he instantly became the center of attention. The world over, his celebrity status was equal to anyone. But now standing in front of Coach the parts didn't equal the whole. He had everything that money could buy. He could afford all the things that made you look important. All the leather, all the technology. But he was far from being important. Important he was not.

Travis was a fraud.

Travis was currently the world's best known movie producer, but he was neither real, nor significant.

He was an actor.

And deep down inside he figured his money, his ability to play a part, would save him. But standing in front of Coach you could now see the difference. Travis was wealthy. He had all the affluence that money could buy. Celebrity. Well-known the world over. Rich and famous. But there was one thing he wasn't. And next to Coach you could see it.

He was no athlete.

An athlete realizes defeat is inevitable, but meets it with resilience.

That resilience allows an athlete to struggle long and hard with tragedy, loss, change, or misfortune.

He lives with the outcome. With dignity. He takes full responsibility for his actions.

The athlete's spirit is indomitable. Fighting against all odds becomes part of his collective imagination. An athlete is never crushed by defeat and doesn't exult in victory. The athletic mind never gives up. Because of that, the athlete lives life to the fullest.

Edward Travis tried vicariously to experience being an athlete through an adopted son he tried to call his own, but he was no athlete.

Edward Travis thought he could buy the character he lacked. But by in attempting to do so, he exposed the fact that he didn't have the discipline that it takes.

He lacked the discipline of desire.

And that is the backbone of character.

Travis' height forced him to look up at Coach, but he was looking up at Coach in more ways than that. And Travis knew it. And so did everyone else in the room, including Travis' own lawyers. Coach wasn't acting. He was real. A man with conviction and unbending integrity.

Isn't that the hardest thing for a Christian to do. Forgive? Is that not a gift from God? God has seen fit to return my son. Why? Why did this all happen? I don't know why. But it's a miracle. Weren't my prayers answered? I have to forgive. Forgive. I cannot just honor God with my lips. I must also honor God with my heart.

Coach reached out his arms to Edward Travis.

And they embraced. Travis wept with his face buried in Coach's chest. Like a child would. In between sobs Travis kept repeating, "I'm sorry. I'm sorry."

With his body battered, his jaw cracked, and his ribs still aching, Coach stood and held Travis in his arms. For sixteen years, sixteen years of Coach's life had come and gone. Sixteen years had been spent agonizing over the loss of his son. And now he stood in a hotel room a thousand miles away from his home and forgave the man who was responsible for beating him and stealing his son.

With Edward Travis still in his arms, Coach turned to the others in the room who now found themselves standing. And most of them, like Coach, were fighting back the tears. Struggling to keep his voice steady and firm, Coach turned and spoke to the others.

"Now. Can I see my son?"

"Now can I see Parker?"

CHAPTER TWENTY-TWO

APRIL 5, 2004

MONDAY NIGHT

THE CHAMPIONSHIP

WESTERN PACIFIC VS. PURDUE

For Coach, life was exploration and discovery.

Unconditional love.
When Parker was born, Coach discovered love. Before Parker the world was still flat.

Responsibility.
Until Parker. Uncharted waters.

Joy.
Because of Parker. More new land was discovered.

Fear.
Before Parker? No such country.

Courage.
It takes real courage to be a father. Obviously, not all men possess it. But those that do see new worlds. Experience awesome wonders. Witness miracles.

Acceptance.

Through Parker, Christ had found Coach. Because of it, Coach discovered who he was. Who he belonged to. Now he understood these discoveries as gifts. Gifts that came from God's grace.

Forgiveness.

This was Coach's newest discovery. Coach knew that like love, it has to be unconditional. It has to be found within. It takes time. But Coach found forgiveness to be key. He forgave Edward Travis. And because he did, Coach was now free to live and explore the world again.

Belief?
Believing?

For Coach it now couldn't be stronger if he had watched Lazarus walk out of the tomb himself. He was about to see his son, who he had lost for almost sixteen years, play for the national championship.

The game was anything but academic.

But it started out that way. Western Pacific jumped out to a 20-6 lead 5 minutes into the game. On treys and press steal layups the Pirates scored 20 quick points in the first three minutes.

But Purdue called a time-out and began to settle down. They were a solid senior laden club, without as much flash as Western Pacific, but they played with composure and with too much confidence to fold during an early run.

The Purdue Boilermakers were the most experienced team in Division I basketball this year. They were a team with eight seniors who were now playing in their fourth straight NCAA Tournament. Five senior starters was a rarity in Men's Division I college basketball today. That peculiarity alone made them a sentimental favorite by sportswriters and college hoop fans all around the country. Purdue had opted for recruiting players they expected to be around for four years. Possibly they would even graduate. No McDonald's hot-shots dreaming of NBA riches. They were locally recruited and their strength was in their cohesion and solidarity.

The Boilermakers regrouped and began to chip away with backdoor and baseline flex cuts for easy baskets. Western Pacific began to show some signs of frustration as their early lead dissipated. The Pirates starting committing reaching fouls and taking closely contested shots.

Slowly, Purdue began to show more poise against the WPU press. Methodically reversing the ball. Barely beating the ten second back court count. They were also beginning to show more patience in their own half court sets. Setting multiple baseline screens, looking for good shots and open cutters. Adding to the Pirates distraction was the fact that many of the Boilermaker scores were now coming seconds before the shot clock buzzer sounded. Purdue was effectively slowing the game down by playing solid ball control basketball.

Today's game seemed to be about highlights. Young players all wanting the highlight. The dunk, the trifecta, followed by pretentious self-promotion. It was all young players practiced anymore. Or cared about. The dunk. The three. It had changed basketball. Changed the players. Changed their attitudes.

Coach thought of it as limiting, but it was definitely the way Western Pacific liked to play. They were new age. New wave. One on one. Bust a move. "You can't guard me!" You didn't see basketball shoe commercials on TV expounding on the virtues of team play. Show companies sold individual intimidation, swagger and self-absorption.

Whenever Western Pacific faltered, it was usually to a team that managed to control the frantic, furious, and conceited pace at which the Pirates preferred to play. They struggled against teams that kept their composure, remained undaunted and unimpressed with the exploits of singular accomplishment and displays of self-indulgent gratification.

Purdue stayed focused. They were getting back on defense, slowing the Pirates down and turning it into a half court game. The Boilermakers were demonstrating what everybody believed coming in; they were a sound veteran team. They had shown they had a chin, could take a punch, and now their patience and experience had gotten them into the late rounds. Their stamina and grittiness were now controlling the fight. WPU was on the ropes.

The Boilermakers caught, and passed the Pirates.

The score at half-time was Purdue 44, Western Pacific 40.

Joanie and Coach were joined by Michelle and her husband, who both had flown in late Sunday night. They all had good seats. Edward Travis had seen to that. They sat in the very back row of the first tier, almost at center court. Edward Travis was up above in a private corporate box. He invited them to join him, but they chose to sit together in a block of four seats in the arena.

Sara and Brian weren't quite as lucky.

The only two seats Travis' people could come up with were on the end of the court, under the basket in the Western Pacific student body section. From where Coach was sitting he could see the two of them sitting right in the middle of the Pirate cheering section, amidst students mostly all clad in purple and gold. They definitely stood out, but knowing Sara, she would make the best of it and probably would have some funny stories afterward to go along with the experience. Besides, the only alternative was to share a box with Travis, and there was no way they both were about to do that.

Last night after Michelle and her husband arrived, the six of them had gathered for dinner at a small Tex-Mex restaurant that sat out overlooking the River Walk.

They shared some quiet conversation about the meeting earlier that day with Travis. And they shared some laughs too, courtesy of Sara who split a bottle of wine with Joanie and Michelle. They were entertaining to say the least. Offering ideas on a variety of creative punishments that should be reserved for Edward Travis. Sara was never afraid to speak her mind anyway. She felt, among other much more colorful things, he should "have his ass hung out to dry." Joanie and Michelle were in total agreement.

Brian was in Coach's corner.

He was realistic and felt Coach and the Bureau had done the right thing. Edward Travis would have been a very difficult man to prosecute and convict. He would hire some of the best defense trial lawyers in the country. Get postponement after postponement, dragging on an impending trial forever. By giving Travis immunity, they would be able to act swiftly, possibly making arrests down in Mexico within the week and hopefully be able to put some "very bad hombres" away for good. He was optimistic that his task force could blow this thing wide open putting an end to the whole frightening "abduction-adoption" business in the U.S.

One thing they all agreed on was that this thing was an absolute media time bomb waiting to go off. Dirty laundry. Dirty laundry wasn't just a huge business in the U.S. anymore. It had become a chief export the world over.

The thunderstorm was going to arrive at the beginning of next week. Brian and Sara were prepping Joanie and Coach on just how much damage could be produced. They expected it to be a blizzard of enormous proportions. A worldwide tempest. Their lives would probably never be the same. And the typhoon was about to engulf the little town of Empire within the next week. Paparazzi from everywhere would be raining down onto their little berg. They discussed some strategies that they might consider to better weather the turbulence.

Brian and Sara were working with Travis' lawyers on setting up a press conference, probably to convene as early as Tuesday of next week.

Brian's task force was only allowing itself one week to get the info they needed to follow it up and make their arrests. They knew if they took longer than that, these people would all have new identities and be long gone.

They would all have to be at the press conference. Even Michelle. It was the only way to allow all the news and media people access to get out the basic info and to answer some questions to at least get a start on satisfying everyone's curiosity. It wasn't going to stop the phone from ringing or photographers from hiding in the bushes, but it would take care of most of the mass media. The newspapers and TV. Afterwards, Brian suggested it might not be a bad idea to plan a vacation, like Hawaii maybe. Sara thought there might be a way get the government to even foot the bill.

Coach couldn't remember the last time he enjoyed a meal so much.

Was it before Parker? How many years has it been since I've seen Joanie laugh? She's teasing me. Touching me. Holding me. I'm laughing. When was the last time I laughed? Really laughed? I'm even funny tonight. Relaxed. Silly. I've got my family back. I did the right thing. I really think I did the right thing. I think Joanie might even think I did the right thing!

Coach, every once in a while, would even catch Michelle looking at him, studying him. He felt like her father tonight. Her real father.

But there was still one thing missing.

Parker.

The wait was killing him. But he figured he waited this long, he could wait until Tuesday. Patience! He certainly didn't want to blow it with Parker. He didn't want to start wagering too much on one hand now that he was ahead. He wanted to make sure he left a winner.

Brian and Edward Travis had agreed to set up a meeting with Parker, Joanie and Coach sometime on Tuesday. Tomorrow! Edward Travis said he would be able to get Lester to remain behind after the team returned to California. As much as the wait was killing him, Coach agreed. Wait until after the championship. Don't pile anymore pressure on Parker than was necessary! He was dealing with enough as it was.

Who knows how he is handling this? He's so young. How's he going to handle this? It's anyone's guess. If I can just talk to him . . .

Coach could barely handle the situation himself. The anticipation. The tension. And he didn't have to play the most important game in his life.

But he was doing a lot better than Joanie. She had her own doubts, concerns and protests. She just wasn't buying in to all the aspects of the game being more important than reuniting Parker with them. She wanted to see her son, and the waiting was getting unbearable for her. She was less cautious than Coach. She wanted to see Parker right away. Forget the game. To her it just wasn't that important.

As disconcerting as it was, it seemed like all afternoon Joanie and Coach couldn't help reminiscing about Parker. The smell of his hair. Some of the funny things he used to say. The games he used to make up. Playing for hours, and always changing the rules. They talked about how hard it was going to be not to want to hold him. To grab him. Squeeze. Squeeze him. Hug him.

The impending reunion was driving them both crazy. Tried as they may, they couldn't help making it harder on themselves by conjuring up fond memories they both shared in regard to Parker.

Purdue scored the first seven points of the second half, forcing Western Pacific to call a time-out.

The Pirates walked slowly toward their bench, heads were down. They had come so far, and having arrived they were expecting to win the Championship. Now there was definitely a look of concern on their faces, they were all looking at Parker. Hoping. Could he save them again?

They're wondering if Parker can work his magic. Yet again? The kid's hurting. They don't know. They might have to save themselves this time.

Coach couldn't help going back to the notion that some how the outcome of this tournament was going to play a role in the outcome of their first meeting. He started agonizing over the consequences again. The game. The score. Coach couldn't help feeling like this team, Parker's team, was not going to be satisfied with getting there. Content with the journey itself. There didn't seem to be a bigger picture for them. They were too pretentious. It was all or nothing.

Do his teammates know? Why didn't I think to ask Travis that? They all might end up blaming him. Would they blame Parker? It wasn't his fault. "Don't blame him. Blame me if you have to blame someone. Why don't you finger-pointers just win the dang game! You've got more talent than they do!"

Coach was ringing wet now. Same ol', same ol'. Game day. Couldn't help himself. He was pretty much unable to talk to Joanie, Michelle, or her husband. He was trying to be polite, but it wasn't very easy. He was making all kinds of coaching adjustments in his head. Getting angry. Thinking about what he would do in this situation, what he would tell the Pirates during the time-out.

Of course, adding to Coach's agitation was the indifference he felt from Joanie. The outcome of this particular event was not at the forefront for her. For Joanie there were obviously more momentous and immediate issues that were paramount to the outcome of any basketball game. Including this one. And she was probably right! Again!

But not for Coach. And he couldn't help feeling resentful.

It's the curse of competition. My obsession with winning. Blessing or a curse? Look at Joanie. It's so easy for her. To her it's just a game. A game! It's never just a game for me. Never was. Probably never will be.

Before Parker was born, Joanie and Coach used to play mixed doubles in tennis tournaments.

But eventually his temperament put an end to it. He just didn't possess the proper disposition for "spouse doubles." He was way too serious for Joanie. Way too competitive. Joanie got incensed over his inability to handle elimination from a tournament.

She found his reaction abhorrent.

He wanted to practice, take lessons, join a club, break down the tape, scout the next opponent. A tennis match? He couldn't have fun. He couldn't enjoy himself. Joanie was right again!

But to Coach there were a lot of positives. After all, wasn't his obsession to win part of the reason he found Parker? His drive. His determination. His willingness to take a risk. Wasn't that some kind of competition?

Either way, Joanie and Coach's views on competition differed greatly. And remained a mystery to both.

Compete! The will to compete. Coach loved heroic effort. He felt they came in all different sizes. Had different scales. Were performed on many different stages. Were performed by many people in many walks of life.

What makes up a hero? Coach had his own definition.

They seem to come up with extraordinary performances when the stakes are the highest.

Heroes don't get unnerved when the pressure is too excruciating for everyone else. The pressure is actually welcomed.

Recognized as a necessary element to finally put themselves to the test. The call comes. And they answer.

"Am I as good as everyone says I am? As tough as I think I am?"

"Now I have the opportunity to find out."

The excitement of venturing into the unknown, forced to play at a higher level with the most at stake, can be so demanding, so intense, so profound, most players can't even stand to watch let alone perform.

Heroes celebrate the moment. Center stage.

"Finally! Trials and ordeals. Endorsement by fire! A venture that will separate me from the rest."

"This is it!"

"The one I have been waiting for all my life. The one I've been dreaming about ever since I was young and discovered I had a gift."

It's sudden. Always unexpected. But you can't let the shock, that realization that everything is on the line, derail you. In an instant you must reach out and grab it. Seize it. Carpe diem. You never know if it will come again.

Most athletes toil in obscurity. They play their whole life hoping, praying, for at least that one chance to rise above.

To wear the crown. To get the ring.

Unfortunately, sometimes, most of the time, it never comes. Even renowned players are forced to retire with that one blemish on their legacy.

"Records? Great! Longevity? Congratulations! No championships? Sorry. No respect."

That is the world we now live in.

For years expectant heroes work to prepare themselves. They have played it out many times before in their own minds while in their driveways and backyards or on the playgrounds. In an empty gym, after practice, when everyone else has already packed up their equipment and left. At home. In their bedrooms. Lying on their backs staring at the ceiling with a ball in their hands . . . 5-4-3-2-1. . . . It's all stored in there, hoping that some day. . . .

And then it happens!
And it is awakened. It is remembered.
It comes alive.
"Oh, I have been waiting for this!"

Sports fans are drawn to it. Enriched by it.

To the sports fan, it is a glorious piece of art, poetry, music or literature. It is an actualization. It transcends social boundaries, social stratification, age and sex. For a moment all of us feel the incurred weight of life itself lifted off our shoulders. It allows us to feel alive and fresh again. It enables us to reach down into our own imagination and feel the joy of dreams and creative expression.

Parker Peterson scored the next twelve points of the game.
It gave Western Pacific a 1 point lead.
He soared through two Purdue time-outs, and two TV time-outs. Two three-pointers were sandwiched around a steal layup, two free-throws, and a baseline jumper.
His defensive determination was epidemic. An infectious fever that fueled Pirate stops and quarantined the Boilermakers from the boards.
Parker was simply not going to let them lose.
Losing was no longer an option.
It was win time. It was his time.

The Peterson curse of competition!

Once the Pirates regained the lead, you could see some self doubt finally begin to creep into Purdue's game.
The Boilermakers went to a junk defense after the last time-out.
A box and one on Parker.

Purdue might have practiced the box and one, but it was obvious that particular defense hadn't been game tested. Parker was able to break it down with his ball handling, and make passes to wide open cutters or three-point spot up shooters.

By the time Purdue abandoned the box and one, Western Pacific had a 9 point lead.

The Pirates broke away.

Purdue was as tough as an oak knot. But they finally cracked. Splintered by crucial turnovers and clock erosion, their quest for immortality was timbered by one unyielding lumberjack.

Long three-point attempts by Purdue were turned into long Pirate outlets and fastbreaks. The fastbreaks were being finished with uncontested layups.

The Western Pacific cheering section began to party. Joanie and Coach got a kick out of seeing Sara and Brian begin to join in on the celebration that was now taking place in the student rooting section. During time-outs, both of them were up dancing and singing with the crowd.

The game ended abruptly.

The margin was too great and there wasn't enough time for the Boilermakers to bother fouling.

Instead the Purdue Coach chose to empty his bench. He began to sub out his senior starters one at a time so they could get a well deserved ovation from the fans.

There would be no senior farewell championship.

There were no tears but more of a mature acceptance. They knew they were done in by a truly astounding athletic performance. They hadn't made history, but they knew they would be part of it.

With a little under 2 minutes to go in the game Parker was subbed for.

Before joining his teammates he went to Purdue's bench and shook the hands of their players and coaching staff. It was a classy thing to do, so unexpected, yet so right. And the entire arena recognized it. They stood and honored the gesture.

Coach lost it.

He couldn't hold on anymore.

He sat leaning forward in his seat staring at the court as the reserves and walk-ons brought the game to a close. He was trying desperately to show some restraint. But he found himself crying. Trying to inconspicuously wipe his face with his sleeves and his hands. Attempting to be nonchalant. Trying not to get caught. He didn't want anyone to see. Especially Joanie. It certainly wouldn't have mattered to her in this case. Maybe it was a conditioned response, fearing her chastisement over yet another extravagant and ardent reaction to a basketball game. He was keeping his head turned away to anyone who tried to talk to him or he felt was looking in his direction.

Joanie spent most of the last few minutes of the game talking with Michelle and her husband. Coach didn't know it at the time, but the small talk was the manner in which Joanie chose to try and control herself. And maybe it was better that way, not allowing themselves any apportionment. Both of them recognized that at this point a potential pouring out of their emotions could leave those around them standing in one big public puddle of sentimental syrup.

Their behavior, of course, was understandable. After all, they were on a course that no one else had ever taken.

They were the pathfinders.

There were no ancient charts rooted in some collective unconscious that could be used to guide their way. No compass. No constant star providing a bearing for their pilgrimage. They were alone. Alone together. Precursors on a voyage of precarious consequence with only an obscure destiny to inflate their sails.

But, to Coach, life was exploration and discovery. Right? Don't turn around! No looking back! Turn the page!

My son. Parker. My son Parker. He just won the National Championship. Not just won it. He was the star. Dominated the game. What! Is this some kind of dream? This has got to be some kind of dream. What a dream! Better than a dream! And nobody knows. Nobody knows. This is my son! That is my boy. My son!

Parker Peterson ended with 33 points and 12 assists.

Parker. Parker. I can say his name over and over and it doesn't hurt anymore. My son! My son! Parker! I wish everybody knew! Seems unfair. But. They will. They will.

There was a tug on Coach's shoulder.
A man was standing in the aisle and handing something to him. A security person.
"Mr. Peterson?" he asked.
"Yes. Yes. That's me. I'm Mr. Peterson," Coach responded looking up at the man from his seat.
It was an envelope. Coach reached out and took it. The security guard turned and headed up the aisle. Coach looked at it. It had his name scribbled on it. "Pete Peterson." He showed it to Joanie and he tore open the envelope. Inside was a locker room press pass. There was a note.

Coach Peterson. Could you please meet me in the locker room? It was signed by Edward Travis.

He shared its contents with Joanie, Michelle, and her husband.

Down on the floor the Pirates were celebrating by dancing around in new championship hats and t-shirts. The bands were still playing. Parker was being interviewed by a TV commentator. Most of the upper level fans were now starting to head for the exits.

"Well, go ahead Pete. We'll wait," it was Joanie breaking the silence.

"Are you sure?" asked Coach.

"Go!" Joanie reached over to squeeze his arm. "Go on. We'll be fine."

"You're sure?" he asked again.

Joanie just smiled back at him. She gave his arm a squeeze, then leaned over and kissed him on the cheek.

"Go Pete. Say hi to our son while you're down there."

That possibility expanded his trepidation even more.

Not now. Not Parker. That meeting has already been set up. Gotta be something else. Should ask Sara. Brian. Ask them what they think.

Coach looked down at the pass. Read the short note again. His heart was pounding. He was beginning to tighten up. Pregame jitters. Jump ball!

"OK. I'll go," declared Coach. "Just give me a minute here. Let the team head for the locker room."

I'm not ready for this. Geez. Caught me off guard. I'm not ready for this. Maybe it's just Travis. Travis wants to talk to me. I'm not going to meet Parker. Am I? Not now. Parker. After this game. It's getting hard to believe he is my son. I'm a little intimidated.

There was little time to sit and think about it. He had to go. He finally got up, kissed Joanie, squeezed her hand, leaned over and hugged Michelle and patted her husband on the shoulder. They all wished him luck.

He turned and headed down the aisle.

CHAPTER
TWENTY-THREE

APRIL 5, 2004

LATE MONDAY NIGHT

SAN ANTONIO, TEXAS

ALAMODOME

Five more minutes. That's it. I've been sitting here for almost an hour. Joanie's got to be worried sick. What is this some kind of a joke? Haven't even seen Edward Travis. Haven't heard from him. This is crazy. What? Did he forget? Check your watch. Five more minutes. Five more minutes. That's it.

After receiving Travis' note, Coach made his way down to the main floor.

He waited until the team's managers, staff, and most of the media had finished packing up their equipment. And except for Joanie, Michelle and her husband, Sara and Brian, who came up to join them from their seats in the student section, most of the stands had emptied.

Finding the proper official to approve his access to the locker room area was a bit of a problem, but eventually a security guard escorted him through the tunnel. He took Coach to a vacant hallway down from the team dressing

226

rooms. A single metal folding chair was there and Coach helped himself. The security guard disappeared after saying he would go to the Western Pacific locker room and look for Edward Travis.

With a few intermittent bursts of pacing in between, Coach sat down and tried to remain patient. He had successfully resisted the temptation of wandering around and trying to find where the press might be meeting with the coaches and players. After all, he did have a press pass. But he tried to remain as close to the place the security guard left him so he wouldn't miss Travis. Now that all the noise and activity down the hall was subsiding, the place was getting quiet, lights were being turned out, and Coach was beginning to believe something must have happened. Maybe the guard failed to deliver the message, maybe prevented from doing so by the security surrounding Travis. Coach had been down that road before. Or maybe Travis himself had been derailed. Changed his mind. Whatever. Coach was running out of patience and was worrying about Joanie. The misgiving he had earlier had now been replaced with loathing. When it came to waiting, Coach was never very composed. This was nothing that could aggravate Coach more than having to stand in line.

That's it! Times up. I can't wait any longer. Not fair. Not fair to Joanie and Michelle. They've got to be worried. Times up. I'm outta here.

Coach was sitting hunched over in the chair, staring down at the floor, hands clenched together between his legs. He reached up to remove his glasses and rubbed his tired eyes.

Hopefully Joanie waited for me. Wouldn't blame her if she left. Back to the hotel. Maybe Travis will call. "Oh, so sorry to keep you waiting. Oh, you didn't get my message? Had to leave town. Business, you know. Hey, thanks for buying all that remorse stuff. Saved my butt."

When he opened his eyes he was looking down at a large pair of basketball shoes. He put his glasses back on and slowly got to his feet.

He was looking into the eyes of his lost son Parker.

There was no mistake.
This was his son.

Those eyes. He had his mother's eyes. There could be no mistake. Not with those eyes.

There was also a lot that was his too. Coach wasn't that good looking. Not even close to being as handsome as Parker was. Not even when he was young. Parker's age. He was never as chiseled either, but there were parts of Parker that were like looking into a mirror.

How could anyone deny it? This is my kid. The face! My face! A long time ago. But my face . . . like an old photograph . . . of me.

There was also something else. Besides his appearance. Coach couldn't put his finger on it. A feeling? Some kind of awareness? A sensation? Whatever it was, Coach knew. It was more than just similar features. More than just those eyes. There was something else. And whatever it was, it left all lingering doubts behind. This was definitely Parker. His son.

How many nights did I lie awake thinking the worse? Parker was dead. Until now I couldn't even say that word in reference to Parker. Dead. Dead? The only way I could picture that, even consider, that was to imagine him in heaven. Waiting for me.
Waiting to say "Dad." "Dad," a hundred times an hour. All I could do was think of him at peace. In heaven. Happy in heaven.
Spared of all the hardships and heartbreaks of life.
The loss of love. Hate. Jealousy. Disenchantment. Hopelessness.
He would never have to suffer the disappointment of love and trust, or the breakdown of a marriage ending in guilt, anger, and

frustration. He would be avoided the depression and sorrow that comes with having to bury your parents. He would never have to struggle with the physical and mental erosion that comes with old age. And he would never have to suffer the pain of having to bury a child. I painted that picture. Only then could I accept Parker having perished.
But Parker is alive. My boy. He's here. He's alive!

"Peterson? Mr. Peterson?"

Parker's question startled Coach. He was still dealing with the absolute realization that it was all true. Scrutinizing Parker as if he were a picture, or a poster. Not real and in person.

But he was not just staring at Parker; he was staring at himself as a young man. He could have stood there transfixed for hours. Gawking. He was much too startled and amazed to answer at first.

Great first impression! I'm standing here like an idiot. Staring at him. Did I hear him speak? That voice. I want to hear it again. It's changed. Deep. Well, what did you expect you idiot? He's not three anymore. Talk! Say something!

"Yes. Yes. I'm sorry," Coach finally managed to blurt out.

Coach wasn't the only one with a growing sense of wonderment. Amazed by the miracle he was witnessing.

Parker was suddenly realizing the same thing.

Unbelievable.

At first Parker had refused to believe the story. Of course, it did confound the wildest of imaginations. But now! Now that he stood in front of Coach, he also recognized, as strange as it seemed, it was all true.

Now they both stood studying each other unable to talk.

"My father." Parker stopped in mid sentence. "Edward." He paused again. "Edward Travis told me the story. At first I didn't believe it. I couldn't. I mean it was way too weird. How could. . . ?" His voice trailed off.

Now they were both struggling to speak.

Both mesmerized.

Hypnotized. Marked by the incompressible idea that doubles do exist.

Coach desperately wanted to hug.

To hold.

The urge was unruly. Drunk and disorderly.

The tears. They were getting so reckless lately. Under the influence. They wanted to come out again too.

Control! Control yourself! You're needed here! Steady. Steady.

"Great . . . game," Coach finally stumbled out. "Con . . . gratulations."

It was soft, it squeaked a little, but Coach managed to get it out. He was relieved to remember there had been a game. It gave him something to say. He almost forgot. The game! It had become a vague recollection. Something that happened long ago, in another lifetime.

Coach reached out to shake his hand. Parker finally looked down and noticed his extended hand and was forced to hesitate a few seconds before being able to reach out and take it. It was difficult to move. Difficult to talk. Spellbound. Neither one able to take his eyes off the other. They were trying not to be impolite, but their enchantment was much too potent to bother with courtesy.

I'm touching him! My son! I'm touching him! How many years? How many years? I can't . . . too much . . . I can't. . . .

"Thanks," Parker was still looking down at Coach's hand. Coach suddenly realized he was shaking too vigorously and too long.

"I'm sorry about the timing," Coach said as he finally let go. "I apologize for that. You're obviously a remarkable young man. Under the circumstances, it probably wasn't easy."

They stood and studied each other some more. Only a few seconds of silence passed. It seemed much longer. Uncomfortable and awkward. Both of them were trying desperately to recover their balance.

Suddenly they both simultaneously shared a chuckle. It was spontaneous and they both ending it by sharing a smile and relieving some of the tension.

It was Parker who finally spoke. "It was a little scary there for a while. The game, I mean. Tonight."

"Well, you can't have a great comeback unless you fall behind," Coach used one of his favorite clichés. "They're going to be talking about your performance for a long time, kid."

"I think they're going to be talking about both of us for a long time, Parker added. He found it was easier to speak if he looked down a little, away from Coach's face. "This whole thing sounds like a movie or something. Maybe something my dad, I mean Ed, could cash in on. Maybe he could find a way to get some mutilation, some gory stuff, and some nudity, into the thing."

They again shared a chuckle.

A sense of humor! The kid likes to laugh. He can laugh at a time like this?

"There's probably a lot of people that are going to want a piece of us, huh? Probably going to get a little crazy," Coach said.

Parker looked back up at Coach and they again shared a smile.

There's just too much. Too much I want to say. To explain. To. . . .

"But something tells me you're going to be able to handle it," Coach added.

Parker was looking down again but nodding in agreement. "I think you're right. I, I mean about the crazy stuff. It's going to be a pain, huh? I guess we don't have much of a choice."

Parker looked up. They both stood for a moment sharing another smile. They were both starting to feel better, informal, despite the lapses in conversation and the problem with articulation. Something was happening. Unbeknownst to the two of them, with no initiative on their part, they were being reconnected. Already beginning to fuse. To link. The light hadn't been turned on in a long long time, but the wiring and all the circuits were still sound.

Parker broke the silence. "Well, I guess I better get going. Team dinner." He slowly backed up a few steps before stopping. There was a part of him that just wanted to leave, get this over with, the whole meeting being so troubling, but there was a part of him that wanted to stay too. And he didn't quite understand why. "It was, ah, nice meeting you. Mr. Peterson."

Parker stood looking back at Coach for a second and then took a step back towards him and reached out to invite another handshake.

Coach had a hard time letting go. Again. This time Parker didn't seem to mind as much. Wasn't as alarming as the first time.

Parker smiled. "Well, gotta go," he said as they both finally let go of each others hand. He slowly turned again to leave.

That smile. The grin. It's a Peterson grin!

"Hey!" Coach blurted out. "Hey congratulations again. Championship! MVP! Wow! You should be proud."

Parker, now some ten feet away, turned back around and looked at Coach once again.

"Thanks." That familiar mischievous grin came across Parker's face again. He looked down again and spoke quietly, mystically, almost as if he were talking out loud to only himself. "You know, I don't know what happened out there. Everything just sorta began to slow down. Eventually, I didn't feel a thing. Pressure I mean. Finally it was just me. No noise. No crowd at all. Didn't seem like I was even aware of my teammates. Just me. Out on the floor. By myself. With all the time in the world." Suddenly Parker caught himself. His head snapped upright. Looked at Coach with consternation. Mouth beginning to fall open. Self-conscious again. A sudden flash of embarrassment. And then, in an instant, it was gone. Followed by the unexpected revelation that Coach knew exactly what he was talking about. He continued to look up at Coach and the Peterson grin slowly resurfaced. "Guess we might be made of the same stuff. Huh?" Parker continued to stand for a moment, half turned, grinning, before turning around again to leave. He stopped. Turned back to face Coach a third time. Coach was still standing in the same spot, too rocked by what he had just heard, much too stoned to move.

Parker spoke. "You know I had this dream last night. Couldn't sleep very well. But when I finally fell asleep. I had this dream. Crazy dream. I was young. A little boy. A little guy. I was playing on the beach somewhere. Jumping and running from the waves. Someone was sitting on the beach laughing at me. I looked up to see who it was. It was you. It was you, sitting on the sand. Crazy, huh?" A smile rising again on Parker's face. "It wasn't a dream, was it?"

Coach looked down and shook his head. Now those inconsiderate, convict tears he was so desperately trying to keep imprisoned, hailed another opportunity to obtain their freedom.

"No. No it wasn't," Coach said barely audible. He looked back up at Parker. He couldn't help himself now. Tears again. Surprisingly, only a single tear escaped, and ran down his cheek.

Coach was surprised Parker didn't seem embarrassed. Instead of being flustered he continued to gaze at Coach, a curious grin on his face. "Hey," he finally asked. "I read your bio on the internet. Said on there they named a gym after you."

Coach nodded again. Finding himself once again trying to use his hands to inconspicuously apprehend tear fugitives that were now threatening to incite a full on prison insurrection. Jailbreak.

Parker was childlike. "Maybe sometime I could visit? You could show me the place? Your gym?"

"I'd like that," Coach said, fearful now of a complete abdication as warden of his emotions. The prisoners were about to be handed over the keys to their cells.

Control! Control yourself! You old fool!

"I'd like that very much," Coach managed.

Steady Peterson. Steady.

"I would. I'd like that very much," Coach succeeded in repeating.

Not now. Not in front of Parker. It's like you just met him. Don't scare the kid. Keep it together! Keep it together!

"OK then. I'll call you. I will. I'll call," Parker declared.

Parker was relieved to see a smile now become part of Coach's disposition, satisfied that they must be tears of joy, he slowly turned and walked down the hall.

CHAPTER
TWENTY-FOUR

AUGUST 19, 2004

THURSDAY MORNING

BLACKTOP COURTS

OUTSIDE THE PETERSON GYMNASIUM

"Are you going to stay out there the whole game? Shooting those bombs?" said Parker, as he retrieved another one of Coach's missed shots.

"That's right hot-dog. Gonna show you some real NBA range. Dunking. That's easy stuff." Coach was trying to get the trash talk out in between trying to catch his breath. "So what do you have now? H-O? Pressure's on now." He was working up a sweat. It was ninety degrees outside and even hotter on the blacktop.

"Probably the only shots you'll get playing for Milwaukee anyway, Parker. Might as well practice 'em." It was Edward Travis, chiming in from his seat on the sidelines. He was referring to Milwaukee's yet unsigned number one pick in the NBA draft—Parker Peterson. Parker Peterson had left college early and became a lottery pick in June's NBA draft.

Milwaukee. Wisconsin. Ironic.

Edward Travis was sitting with Joanie, Michelle, and Parker's girlfriend Lorie, at a patio table set up next to the court. They were sipping lemonade and ice tea covered by the shade of a large umbrella.

Also sitting with them was a writer for *Sports Illustrated.* The magazine's photographer was buzzing around taking photos of everyone.

"Let the kid win, you old geezer. You're supposed to help build your kid's self esteem. At least give him some confidence until he gets to Wisconsin. There he'll find out he's the smartest person in the state." Joanie's comments got a big laugh from everyone sitting around the table, including the sportswriter.

"Don't listen to 'em trash my home state, Parker. The Cheeseheads are the greatest fans in the world," Coach said as he airballed a thirty-footer.

"They're mosquito food. The mosquitoes are so big there, Parker, they wear t-shirts that say "I LOVE OFF." That one came from Michelle, and also got a lot of laughs.

"No sir, my job is to deflate the ego of Mr. Number One Draft Pick," Coach said as he moved into position to rebound Lester's shot.

"Not going to happen," Parker said as he took aim from thirty five feet out. "How do you say 'Signing Bonus'?" The shot swished.

Coach failed to duplicate the shot from high above the top of the arch. "R."

Again Parker from deep in the corner. "How do you say 'Shoe Contract'?" Swish. "Feeling the pressure now, Dad?"

Parker's father missed the long shot from the corner. "S."

"How do you say, Oh man, it's cold out here! My car won't start! How am I going to get up Nort' for deer hunting?" Edward Travis' comment got big laughs from everyone, including Coach.

Parker again from way out. "How do you say 'Rookie of the year'?" Again, swish. The patio furniture group began to hoot and holler.

"What do you have now? H-O-R-S?" Parker asked.

"Yeah. How do you say, Lights out for the old geezer?" Joanie getting two more cents in.

Coach clanged it off the back of the rim. "E." Game over.

"You're right, Joanie. What kind of dad wouldn't let his son win once in a while?" Coach said as he trotted over to take a sip from his glass of ice tea.

"Come on Dad. Track time," Parker announced as he padded Coach on the back. "Let's go. You can't shoot. Maybe you can still run a little."

"OK. OK. You're gonna kill me kid," Coach said wiping the sweat from his face with a towel.

"You might want to practice jogging in snow boots carrying a snow shovel, Parker," Edward Travis said as Parker and Coach turned to jog across the blacktop. "Jogging on the frozen tundra." Edward Travis was trying to do an imitation of sports caster Chris Berman's SportsCenter reference to the Green Bay Packer stadium, Lambeau Field. Chris Berman invariably referred to the Packer home field as the "frozen tundra."

Parker and Coach shared a laugh between themselves as they headed across the blacktop. They purposely bumped shoulders as they headed through the gate and out onto the track.

Laughing. Laughing together.

For the past week Parker and Coach had been together.

Inseparable. Kindred spirits.

They biked, ran and lifted weights. In between they looked at old photos and family videos.

Coach showed him pictures of his teams. Told him stories. Coach was a storyteller again.

The three of them, Joanie, Coach and Parker, went out to eat.

They went to the movies.

Or Coach and Parker laid in lawn chairs in back of the house and soaked up rays while talking about anything. And everything.

On Thursday Edward Travis flew in with Lorie. Coach was so impressed with Lorie, Parker's girlfriend. A collegiate golfer with her own professional aspirations. They had all agreed to get together for a *Sports Illustrated* exclusive. The first and only magazine exclusive they all agreed to do together. They were all part of Parker's family now.

And it felt good. Parker was alive again. And so was Coach.

Coach noticed everything.

The song of the birds out back. The deer that walked quietly through the woods.

Where had all these thing gone?

The roses.
Taste. Food had taste again.
The smell of fresh coffee.
A warm summer breeze.
And Joanie!
Everything about Joanie.
Her beauty. Her smile. Her touch. The smell of her hair.

And when he laughed. when he noticed himself laughing, sometimes he would start to cry. Laughter brought tears. It had been a long time since he laughed. Really laughed.

Friends stopped by to visit. Michelle and her husband came for dinner. Brought pizza. Coach Dutroy stopped by. Brought a pie. Joanie's family came over with her brothers and sisters; they all had picnics out on the deck. Went to the river. Swam.

The computer? The internet? Coach kicked that habit.

He read voraciously. Books, magazines, newspapers. And he wanted to talk about it all. Share everything. He couldn't stop talking.

No cynicism. No bitterness. No jealousy or anger. All vanquished. Jettisoned. And in their place. Trust. Faith. Devotion.

He watched TV. And he would laugh at the dumbest shows.

And Michelle.

He couldn't get enough of her. Called her on the phone just to say hi. He never called her on the phone. He wanted to be part of her life again. And she was pregnant! A grandfather! He would be the best grandfather.

Maybe if Parker marries Lorie, more grandkids!

The sky was blue. The grass was green. The wind blew. And Coach noticed it all.

As they circled the track Parker asked Coach about being baptized in his church. Maybe even join on Sunday. This Sunday! He wanted to go with Coach.

More blessings? Just keep 'em coming! Wow!

Together they circled the track. Now Parker was chatting away about something. But Coach was having a hard time listening.

He was saying a silent prayer.

You are the vine . . . I am the branch . . . I abide in you . . . as you have abided in me. . . .

He was counting his blessings. Saying thanks. Thankful. Thankful for his greatest blessing of all.

The blessing of being a father.

A father to a son.

ABOUT THE AUTHOR

Growing up in Wisconsin, Craig Strohm filled his days bouncing around baseball sandlots, football fields and driveway basketball courts. Sandwiched between those seasonal skirmishes, he spent his time reading and writing. His love for literature grew as deep as his love for sports and competition. He graduated from the University of Wisconsin, Stevens Point, in 1973 with a teaching credential and moved west. For the past twenty-five years he has taught high school English and Social Studies in Grass Valley, California.